nudged

nudged

a story

by

G Hartmore

Harmonik Publishing
Williamsport, PA, USA
www.harmonikpublishing.com

ISBN: 098964300X
ISBN-13: 978-0989643009
LCCN: 2013916539

to Aunt Gerri,

…who always believed.

"Coincidence is God's way of staying anonymous"

--- Albert Einstein

PART
ONE

Chapter 1

THE END

My father's great-great-grandfather is buried here. His headstone is old and mildewed and weathered, almost beyond recognition. His simple, thin, marble slab stands taller than most in its vicinity. It displays only his name, the date of his death, and the number of years, months, and days that he lived, nothing more. Next to his stone is a bronze-finished War of 1812 military memorial marker sticking up about a foot from the ground with a weathered United States flag imbedded in the notch of the metal. His wife's stone is nearby, as are the tiny marble squares that indicate that two of their infant sons had not lived to be a year old. They were twins it says.

Several yards away, there is another group of monuments led by my father's great-grandfather. His smallish government-provided headstone shows only his name and the unit for which he served during the Civil War. His military marker is planted next to the stone and is also adorned with a worn American flag. His wife's

3

stone and the several small stones of their infant children and grandchildren are located nearby. No other generation of my family is buried here, probably because they lived too long and died too late, their deaths coming long after this cemetery was all but forgotten. I had discovered this holy place by accident, about 20 years ago, during a genealogical search. I don't know if my father ever knew it existed.

This small cemetery and the old stone church across the street are located in the White Deer Valley that is surrounded by the Bald Eagle Mountains in Pennsylvania. They are situated on a small parcel of the land that was taken over by the federal government, over 70 years ago, for its use as a huge prison complex. Most of the area's buildings were torn down, but for some unknown reason, this church and cemetery were left intact. Through an ironic agreement, they are cared for and preserved by the prison populations.

The air always seems cleaner here. I close my eyes and roll back my head, breathing in the cool breeze as it caresses my face. This is my haven, my sanctuary. For many years now, I've come here to recharge my soul, but I know now that its powers are not enough anymore. I feel exhausted and numb, and I realize that my despair has finally won. This is my end.

There are three wooden benches located on the fenced-in property of this meagerly populated cemetery, and I occupy the middle one. The fence is composed of two long, black metal bars attached to brick pillars every 10 feet or so and two taller brick pillars that support a metal gate at the entranceway. Even though no new grave has been dug here for some 50 years now, the church and cemetery seem well kept up and are mowed and trimmed neatly by the prison crews that apparently visit here about once a week during the growing season. The fence was put up after the government had taken over, and the benches were added even later. My bench is in quite good condition, although its wooden slats could use a coat or two of paint, and the iron legs are a bit rusty. There are trees all around the fence line and a small grove inside, near the middle. I am quite comfortable sitting here, even if the occasional late day breeze makes it seem a bit chilly.

It's quite a bit colder here than down south where I had most recently lived, but the hooded sweatshirt does its job well, and the stocking cap keeps my ears reasonably warm. I left most of my other possessions in a local storage unit that my father had rented, and I have continued to maintain after his death. I did bring a container of hot coffee to help keep me warm and alert, but I haven't opened it yet. Next to it on the bench, I've placed the olive drab t-shirt whose sole purpose has always been to wrap and protect my father's .45 caliber handgun. Lying next to it is the matching magazine, loaded with 8 compatible bullets.

Although I do have some distant relatives that live fairly close to this valley, I have never actually met any of them. They probably don't even know that I exist. As a child, I traveled and relocated at the whims of my father's military duty. Later, my own military service kept me from settling down here or in any other familiar place. I've never stayed in one place long enough to really call it "home". It is to here that I feel drawn, to this place that I have never lived, but where many of my family's generations have lived and died and eventually were forced out. It is here that I feel most at home. Fittingly, this is also the place where I choose to die.

I am tired, and I feel more alone than ever. My thoughts are dominated with guilt and depression, and I sob silently in confession to whatever Deity that will listen. I've aged out of the military, and now I'm unable to keep my head clear long enough to give meaning to my life after I "retired". I've looked for some reason to justify my existence, my reason to live, but I always seem to come up lacking. There are no more wars for me to fight, no more soldiers to mentor, and no family to raise. These were always the distractions that allowed me to temper the guilt and emptiness that now dominate my thoughts every day.

When I am found in this cemetery, probably by a passing caretaker, no one will know who I am, and no one will care. From the identification in my wallet, the authorities may connect my surname to a couple of the old headstones, but since my father and grandfather are not buried here, they will not be able to connect the timeline.

I first found my father's handgun when I was a young teenager, rummaging through his retired military foot locker while reveling in his smells. It was a fully loaded .45 caliber piece which held a much higher level of fascination for me than the single shot .22 caliber rifle I was given at Christmas. Its magazine was full, but it had a trigger lock that kept me from doing something stupid. I never did fire that gun, nor any other handgun until well into my own military career when I was training for some random security detail.

Yesterday, I found his gun again when I was looking through some of the boxes he left behind in storage when he died over 20 years ago. I had never even bothered to look inside them until then. Most of the contents were pictures, tools, and military paraphernalia. There were several documents inside that had his handwriting, and the smells of pipe tobacco and old uniforms still reminded me of him. He had saved many mementos of me at events that I had all but forgotten. They included my Little League photos, trophies, certificate awards, and even a picture of my mother and him and me at my high school graduation. He always told me that I was destined for greatness, a concept I have long since refuted many times over.

The gun was at the bottom of his stenciled foot locker, wrapped in one of his military issued T-shirts. It was still loaded, but the trigger-lock had been removed. Every piece of it was in like-new condition. My father was, after all, a Marine, and they were conditioned to have everything clean and tidy and ready for action. There was no doubt in my mind that it would fire right away and would continue to fire if needed.

The .45 feels especially cool to my touch as the sun makes its way out of sight of the valley. It feels lighter now than it did when I first discovered it as a youth, and it seems much smaller too. Its metal barrel has traces of oil residue which I wipe off with my thumb, and the wooden grip is shiny and polished. I turn it upside down and look up the magazine chamber and rotate it around to inspect the trigger and the sights. I am delaying because I am afraid. If I aim the gun at my head and pull the trigger, I am afraid of what comes next, maybe nothing at all. I am afraid too, of what life will be like if I am unable to complete this final intention.

I am a coward, and it sickens me. With renewed adrenaline, I grab the magazine and ram it into the chamber, and before I can think, I throw forward the barrel which effectively loads the weapon. And I think that's what my father would say, "It's a weapon, not a gun!" because that's what all good Marines would say. I am delaying again, and I realize that if I can't finish this here and now, I will never be able to finish it again. I understand that if I want to accomplish my mission, I cannot think, I just need to stick it up to my head and pull the trigger, do not think!

I slowly raise the weapon to my temple, but even as it approaches its intended target, I accept that I can't pull the trigger, and I know I'll never have that much courage ever again. I am saddened, and the self-pity washes over me, and I again start to cry. I'm not even sure why I'm such a pitiful mess this time. Is it because I'm such a coward, or is it because of what comes next? With the acceptance of my failure, I am frustrated, and then I am just angry. I fling the gun away in anger and disgust.

The weapon goes off when it hits the side of the closest brick pillar. I feel the bullet hit me, and I feel the burn and the pain. I realize that even though I have probably achieved my original goal, I am still a coward. As I lose consciousness, I wonder what my father would think about me now.

Chapter 2

HOSPITAL VISITATION

Before starting his work week, Judge Valentine Waltman stopped at his mother's house. He dropped off his car in exchange for his father's pickup truck, and he ran inside for a hug from his mom and a quick cup of coffee. Even though his father had been dead for over 20 years now and had bought the truck several years before that, it had held up well despite not having mechanical hands around to keep up its condition. It has had its share of minor bumps and bruises and could probably use a good tune-up, but all things considered, it still functioned well. He needed the truck to transport one of his mother's lawnmowers in the hopes of finding the time to drop it off at a small engine shop for repair in preparation of the rapidly approaching mowing season.

Of course, his mom had used this occasion to remind him to keep looking out for someone who could help out around the house. The Judge had been the house's main caretaker for these many years, even though he had moved out a few years back when he had started his own family. He agreed that she could use the help, and he certainly would like to hand over the daily upkeep tasks of the old farmhouse and its grounds to someone he could trust. But the Judge hadn't found the right person for the job, and quite frankly, he didn't know where else to look.

Today, Judge Waltman's work week was starting out with a trip to the hospital. He had been assigned the case of a retired military man who had apparently attempted suicide in a small remote cemetery in the White Deer Valley on the edge of the county. Army Staff Sergeant Samuel Barto was most recently known to live in Virginia near the base he had retired from. He seemed to have some family roots here as indicated by the matching surnames on the headstones near where he was found. But so far, they hadn't been able to find any local family or friends.

This was an especially interesting case for the Judge. His father had been a veteran, and his family was heavily involved with the local Veteran's Center as volunteers. His assignment was to evaluate Sergeant Barto and find out what to do with or for him. If he was mentally incompetent, or if he was a danger to anyone else, the Judge could legally assign him to the regional mental institution. This county and his family took a veteran's well-being very seriously, but he had never been assigned an attempted suicide before.

Unsuccessful suicide was not technically against the law anymore, and even when it was illegal in the law books of this country, the penalties were rarely enforced. Judge Waltman focused on his mission to see to the "victim's" mental and physical health and to make sure that the people around him were in no danger.

Sheriff Robert Bastian had found Sergeant Barto, unconscious and leaning up against a wooden bench at the Stone Church Cemetery in the valley near the prisons. He had a bullet wound in his upper thigh and was bleeding quite badly. A recently fired .45 caliber handgun was lying next to him. All indications seemed to show evidence of a botched attempted suicide. The Sheriff noted that this was quite an isolated area, and he had just happened to be passing by while visiting the prison grounds. Sergeant Barto's case file was filled with information from many different sources, most of which came from the sheriff's research and Barto's military record.

Samuel Barto had spent 20 solid, if not spectacular years in the Army, and he was now drawing a military retirement pension. He was an auto and truck mechanic and had served in the Persian Gulf War. He had recently moved out of his apartment near Fort Lee, Virginia, and there was no mention of any wife or children. Apparently in his 50 plus years of life, he had no history of mental problems and no indications of why he would have tried to kill himself.

When Judge Waltman entered Sergeant Barto's hospital room the TV was on, but Barto was sitting somewhat upright with his eyes closed. He obviously wasn't sleeping as he stirred and opened his eyes when he sensed another person in his vicinity.

"Good morning Sergeant Barto, I'm Judge Valentine Waltman."

"Good morning sir," replied Barto while looking over the Judge as he was removing his lightweight jacket. It had been a long time since he had been called Sergeant. "Are you here to put me in jail?"

Judge Waltman smiled slightly and shook his

head. "I don't think so, but we do need to talk. Is it okay if I sit down?"

"Yes sir, please do."

From a quick talk with the nurses and his own observation, the Judge formed his first impression quickly. The nurses described Barto as a quiet, sad man who was polite from his years in the military, but apparently also from his upbringing. He didn't talk much to them except when responding to their questions. They told the Judge that no one from the hospital had talked to him yet about his suicidal circumstances, and he had received no visitors. Barto remained silent, and it was obvious to the Judge that he would have to initiate any significant conversation between the two men.

Barto's hands were folded in his lap and bore the dark oil-stained skin tone typical of a longtime auto mechanic. After getting comfortable in his chair, the Judge started. "I see from your records that you live near Fort Lee in Virginia. Are you here visiting family or friends?"

"No sir. I moved out of my apartment in Virginia before I came up here. I've never had any friends here, and what family I had are all gone I guess, although I suppose you could count my family that are in a few of the cemeteries in the area."

"Sheriff Bastian tells me there are other Barto's in the cemetery he found you at."

"My great-great-great grandfather and grandmother are buried there. They were one of the first members of that church. He was a veteran of the War of 1812. My great-great grandfather and grandmother are buried there too. He was a Civil War Vet. A lot of their family is there too."

The Judge could tell by the emphasis Sergeant

Barto made on his family's military service that it was important to him. He was obviously proud of that heritage.

Barto felt the need to explain his more recent generations and their locations so he continued. "My great-grandfather and my grandfather are both buried at Everest. My father is there too. He's in the veteran's section."

The Judge knew Everest Cemetery. It was the largest cemetery in the area, and his father was buried there too, also in the veteran's section. "Do you visit this area often?" asked the Judge.

"My dad died here over 20 years ago. I've tried to get back here at least once a year. I like to go camping when I'm here. It's always so peaceful and quiet. While I'm here, I visit the church and cemetery, and I check on my father's things. He put a lot of his stuff in storage before he died, and I've kept it there." Actually, even though he continued to pay for the rental of his father's storage space, Barto had barely touched any of his father's things until this trip.

"Where are you staying now Sergeant Barto?"

Barto thought carefully about his answer. He had been camping in a nearby state park, but his gear and most of his personal possessions were now in storage along with his father's stuff. "I really hadn't thought much about the future Judge. Since I moved out of my place down south, I don't really have any particular place to go." He dropped his head and stared at his hands. "I guess I'll need to look into that now."

The Judge now decided it was time to start asking the tougher questions. "Sergeant Barto, out at the cemetery, were you trying to kill yourself?"

"Yes sir, Your Honor," Barto replied quietly but

quickly. He didn't want to lie to the Judge, and he knew that the Judge would not have believed him even if he had. He continued with a quick sarcastic chuckle and a slight shake of his head, "The big, bad military man can't even shoot himself right."

The Judge's next instinct was to ask why, but this probably wasn't the time or the place for that, and he wasn't the right person for that type of interrogation anyway. He could arrange counseling appointments at the local VA hospital. Instead, he stayed focused on his duty to Sergeant Barto and the residents of this county.

Before he could ask anything further, Barto answered the Judge's unspoken question, "I guess I'm done with all that Judge. I've already failed, and I can't imagine ever having the nerve to try it again."

The Judge paused in silence as he gave Barto a chance to gather himself after his confession. He thought carefully about his next question to the beaten down military man. "What now then Sergeant Barto? Where do you think you'll go, and what will you do?"

Even though this was the first time he had given any serious thought to those questions, his answer to the first part of the question seemed obvious. "I think I'd like to stay around here if that's okay Judge." Barto felt it appropriate to ask the Judge's permission. "And I'm actually a pretty good mechanic. I'm good with my hands, so I should be able to find a job that can supplement my military pension."

The nurse appeared at the doorway and asked the Judge to step outside while she administered Barto's regularly scheduled tests.

At the door, the Judge said, "Sergeant Barto, I'd like to talk to you some more if that's okay. How about I see if I can get you a pass for this evening, and we'll go out and get some real dinner. We can talk more then."

Barto agreed, as much out of respect for the Judge as anything, but he admitted to himself, a good nonhospital meal did have some nice appeal. "Thank you Your Honor," said Barto as the Judge left the room. Barto was thanking the Judge for the invite, but also for the time he had taken just for him. He wasn't accustomed to being the center of anyone's attention unless it was their duty to do so, and he could feel the personal touch that the Judge had applied.

As the Judge walked down the long hospital corridor, he couldn't help but think about his mom's repeated message to him asking for help around the house and how this veteran handyman was perfectly qualified to fill that role. From the pile of information that Sheriff Bastian had collected and the brief time he had spent with Sergeant Barto, he felt like he had known him for years. He was certain that Barto was no threat to his family, and his mom would certainly welcome him. Maybe fate had stepped in to nudge them together. He smiled as he pulled out his cell phone and dialed his mom's telephone number at the Waltman Estate.

Chapter 3

THE WALTMAN ESTATE

The drive to Susannah Waltman's house started out quiet and perhaps a bit awkward, but the Judge opened up the conversation by describing his mother's farmhouse. He jokingly referred to it as the "Waltman Estate". When he had told Sergeant Barto that they were going to his mom's house for a home-cooked meal, Barto was tentative. It was too late to say no anyway, as the Judge had strategically waited to tell Barto about their destination after they were already in the truck and on their way.

"Mom and Dad moved in about forty years ago, soon after I was born. It was a smaller house then, but they built on as time went by and as our family grew. It used to be a farmhouse. It's been there for over one hundred years. Dad died about twenty years ago, and I try to keep it up as best as I can, but with my own family and the size of the land it's on, I'm having a hard time keeping up." There, he thought, I had thrown out a hint.

"Between this truck, their van, and their cars, sometimes I think I should've gone to school for auto mechanics rather than law, not to mention the mowers and other little pieces of equipment." Okay, there's a second hint thrown out. Time to back off before I overwhelm the poor guy.

Barto was not naïve, nor was he stupid, but he wasn't completely focused, although he was listening carefully. He did notice the connection between his skills and the needs of the Waltman clan, but he had not taken the info from the Judge as a job opportunity.

"Does your mom live alone in the house?"

"No, no, she's always had us around. I lived there until I got married, and my three sisters are still there. I can't imagine them not being together or at least close by, and I only live around the corner. Our family has always been close and got even tighter after Poppy died. We all called my dad Poppy. He was a veteran like you. He was in the Army in the sixties, and when he got out, he joined the Reserves. He flew a helicopter, a medical helicopter, transporting victims and patients. His war was Vietnam, and when he was done there, he did the same thing here as a civilian. He flew an emergency medical transport helicopter around here. He died when he was flying in an Army Reserve training mission while he was on his monthly active duty tour."

Barto had been quiet for some time, but was listening intently. He felt obligated to make some kind of polite comment. "I was too young for Vietnam, but the older guys that I was stationed with used to talk about their time there. One guy always made it a point to say that we didn't lose that war, that we just decided that the cost to win it was too high. I think I know what he meant. We had the firepower to erase all the bad guys in their country, but we didn't use it; too much collateral damage. It made sense when I thought about it."

Barto felt more comfortable when their truck drove up the sloped driveway of the Waltman family house. The Judge parked the truck near a large garage at the back of the house on the edge of the circled driveway. When he noticed the mower still in the back, he remembered that he never did take the time to drop it off for repair. He hoped that maybe he had found another solution. Barto counted the large passenger van and three smaller cars parked inside and noticed very little room for tools or storage, an observation only a mechanic would notice.

Barto's leg felt good enough that he had turned down a cane that was offered at the hospital. He limped along beside the Judge as the Judge pointed at his late-model car in the driveway.

"We'll take my car when we return you to the hospital later."

"What's in there?" Barto asked about a large separate building at the side of the driveway.

"That's Poppy's workshop. You'll appreciate it I think," the Judge said as he detoured toward the shop. The door opened easily, and as he turned on the bright overhead lighting he said, "It's a bit dusty from inactivity, but my dad loved coming out here. He fancied himself an amateur car mechanic and tinkerer."

Inside, the shop had several distinct sections whose functions were obvious at first glance. Straight ahead was the mower and yard work equipment section. There were several push mowers in various states of repair and a riding mower that appeared to be in good working condition. Weed cutters, pruners, and edgers hung on the wall surrounding the bigger equipment along with several shelves of gas and oil cans and other assorted accessories.

To the right was an interior door where the Judge guided Barto. "This was where he spent a lot of his time," the Judge said as he walked into the hands-on section of the workshop. "He had a few tools and benches and a lot of projects. I'm not sure he got a lot done, but he sure liked it out here." He pointed at a dusty but sturdy wooden rocker in the corner near a space heater. "Over there was where Mom would sit. She'll tell you how they used to spend time here talking and just enjoying each other's company. I've often suggested that she bring the chair in the house, or at least to the porch, but she always says it belongs right here where it is."

"Well Sergeant Barto, we better get inside and let Mom know we're here."

As they approached the house, the smells of home cooking were immediate. When they opened the door into the sitting room that led to the kitchen, the Judge smiled and pointed to the chairs and side tables in the wide cove leading to the kitchen and said, "This is our "Room of Souls" Sergeant Barto. Poppy called it that because we all seem to congregate here when we need time to talk or think about good times and even some bad times. There's been a lot of coffee and pie consumed in these chairs and a lot of laughs and some tears too, but it's always been a special comfort zone for our family and friends."

The kitchen and its small dinette were just off the side of the kitchen sitting room. At the open oven door was a short but sturdy white-haired woman, dressed in a freshly pressed dress and apron that would have fit in a 100 year old farm house as easily as it was appropriate today. It was apparent at Barto's first glance that

Susannah Waltman was well suited to the role of matriarch of the family. When she saw them enter, she made a quick inspection of the oven's contents and firmly closed its door. She wiped her hands on her apron and briskly walked over to the pair of waiting men.

Mrs. Waltman started talking before the Judge could spit out any introductions. "Mr. Barto, thank you so much for coming," as she reached up with both hands around his neck and hugged the stiff man. She said upon his release, "Sorry, I'm a hugger, but you'll just have to humor an old lady."

"Thank you for inviting me ma'am," replied Barto with a slight but sincere grin. Barto was not a hugger, but his stiff reaction was more due to lack of practice rather than disapproval. He couldn't remember his last hug, and this one had felt warm and good, and Mrs. Waltman smelled like freshly baked bread.

After she released Barto, she reached for her son. "You get one too Val," to which the Judge replied with a big grin, "I'd better!"

"Dinner will be ready soon Mr. Barto. I hope you like fried chicken," she said.

"It's one of my favorites," Barto replied honestly, "and it smells great." So far so good Barto thought. Although he was always uneasy in a social environment, the Judge and Mrs. Waltman were making it easy to get comfortable.

"Val, take Mr. Barto into the greatroom, and show him around, and introduce him to the girls."

The Judge and Barto began the tour by taking a left-hand turn around the basement entranceway directly across from the kitchen exit. They entered a small but impressive room, lined with books all around with several strategically placed reading chairs and matching floor lamps. In one corner by a window, there was a painter's easel with a high back chair. "Mom and Dad used to sit here in the library after us kids were taken care of for the night. Dad would get a book and Mom would sit at her easel and paint. I still like to come and sit in here when I visit… to absorb the peace and quiet." Barto loved to read, and this room was a definite joy.

Continuing through to the far end of the room, they passed stairs to the upper floor on the right and the front exterior door to the left. "There are four bedrooms and a bathroom upstairs. Mom sleeps in the room out by the kitchen that they had originally added on as a playroom. It's much easier for her to navigate around here without worrying about going up and down the stairs so much." Barto nodded his head in understanding.

There were two women fussing around the big dining room table in the next room. When they saw the Judge and Barto enter, they smiled instinctively and walked towards them. Val introduced the closest lady that approached and gave her a hug. "This is my oldest sister Margaret."

"Oldest sister maybe, but he's still older than me," added Margaret with a grin.

"And this is my youngest sister Sarah," as he hugged the younger woman. "This is my new friend Samuel Barto."

Barto noted the term "new friend" the Judge had used to describe him and wondered if it was truly possible for him to have started a friendship this quickly when he had started out the day with no friends at all; or was it simply the Judge's way of being polite?

Margaret was only slightly taller than her mother, but shared her same strong build. She shook Barto's hand firmly with a strength that reminded him of the female leaders that he had met in the military. "Welcome, Mr. Barto. Val tells us you're an Army veteran. Our dad was in the Army too. Vets are always welcome here."

"Yes ma'am, twenty years and retired. Thank you for having me." Barto made a mental note that the family had been briefed on at least some of their visitor's background and wondered just how much the Judge had told them.

Sarah was several inches taller than both her sister and her mother and shared Val's slender build. With her hand around her brother's waist, there was no question that they were siblings.

"It's very nice to meet you Mr. Barto."

"The pleasure is mine ma'am," Barto answered politely.

Margaret said, "Sarah, why don't you show Mr. Barto the greatroom and introduce the rest of our family. Val and I can finish setting the table."

"This way Mr. Barto," said Sarah as she turned and pointed toward a wide-open room on the other side of the dining area.

There were two very large sofas and various mismatched armchairs surrounding a large screen TV. On one sofa was a young girl and a young boy, both around 11 or 12 years old, and on one of the comfortable looking armchairs was another adult woman who was apparently assigned to chaperone duty.

"Elizabeth is my other sister," Sarah began. "This is Mr. Barto, Val's new friend."

"Well then, he is our new friend too," added Elizabeth. "Rasheem, say hi to Mr. Barto."

"Hi," replied the young boy with a token wave, but without turning away from the TV.

Elizabeth wore her hair short and had a physically

fit body that reminded Barto of a tomboy. "Rasheem is my foster child Mr. Barto," she said, "and Laura is Sarah's daughter. Pardon them please, they love watching movies, and *Dumbo* is one of their favorites."

Barto noted that Rasheem was a skinny black boy who had not yet hit his growth spurt, and Laura was a cute little brunette whose hairstyle and facial features were much like her mother's. Both were entranced with the TV, Rasheem wide-eyed and Laura with a slight but obvious smile covering her face. A big unlit fireplace took up nearly the entire far wall of the greatroom, and the door to a bathroom was on the other side, halfway between the greatroom and the dining room.

The conversation at the dinner table was relaxed and comfortable. What had started out as an evening of dread for Barto had turned into a relaxing time with a cheerful gathering. Small talk about the house, the military, and good food dominated the conversation. Rasheem was fidgety and talkative, while Laura was quiet and politely still. In fact, she hadn't said a word. Barto noticed that the adults talked very generally and never asked him any personal questions. He was at ease here, and the meal was the best he could ever remember.

Val spoke up at the end of the meal, "There's one more area of the house I'd like to show you if your leg is up to some stairs."

"Certainly," Barto replied. His leg was a bit stiff and could use a good stretching.

The Judge commented as he and Barto went down the steps into the basement, "Mom has her laundry room and a pantry over there." As they approached the door at the far side of the basement, Val opened the door and said, "This is what I wanted to show you."

Inside, Barto saw a huge finished bedroom with

several chairs and gooseneck lamps. There was a small refrigerator, a chest of drawers, a clothing armoire, and a king-sized bed, surrounded by two night stands with their own lamps.

"This was my room Sergeant Barto. I loved it in here. It has its own bathroom over there," he said, pointing to a side interior door, "and its own entrance or exit, depending on what mischievous predicament I may have been into at the time. Mom calls this a guestroom now, but I can't remember the last time it was actually used."

Barto noticed how clean and organized the room was for not being used very much. "Very nice Judge, it's kept up well too, for not having anyone in here for so long. Are they hoping you come back to live with them?"

"No Sergeant Barto, my guess is that they were down here cleaning up and dusting in the hopes that they would have a new housemate."

"Samuel, let me get right to the point. My mother has been on me to get her some help around this place, and quite frankly, I'm struggling to help out here and still take care of my own house and family. They need someone to fix things around the house, keep up the vehicles, maintain the landscaping, and stuff like that. There's a lot of work, especially for me with my family. My sisters help out a lot, but they always remind me that this place needs a man's touch."

Barto stood still and silent, absorbing the Judge's story.

The Judge continued, "My mother and my sisters would like to hire you to be the Waltman Estate handyman and caretaker." He emphasized "Waltman Estate" a bit sarcastically, so that Barto knew he was again being playful with that description. "They can't pay you a monetary salary, but they can offer you this room, use of the workshop, and all the food you can handle. To be honest, they're all great cooks, but I believe tonight's "special dinner" was meant as a bribe." The Judge put his hand on Barto's shoulder and said, "You don't have to decide now Sergeant Barto, but I think this would be a great situation for both you and for them."

Barto's mind was racing. He knew that his military retirement pay would give him plenty of spending money since he had no bills per se, especially if he had no rent to pay. But he worried about forcing himself on this family whom he had grown to like in such a short time. He felt unusually comfortable around them, even after knowing them for only a few hours. And then he thought of his most recent actions at his church. Barto spoke quietly with his eyes cast downward. "Judge, do they know why I was in the hospital?"

Susannah Waltman chose that moment to enter the room, and Barto could see all three sisters just outside the doorway. He hadn't noticed them before and wasn't sure how long they had been there. She began, "We know Mr. Barto, and we know you're going through some tough times, but that's okay with us, we've all been through them too, and I'm sure there's plenty more to come."

Margaret spoke up with a playful smile, "It's you who may not want to be around us, once you get to know us."

Elizabeth added, "You'll have as much privacy as you want Mr. Barto, and hopefully the four wacky Waltman ladies won't drive you nuts too much."

Sarah was the last to speak, "Please stay here with us Mr. Barto. It'll be nice to have a man around the house. No offense Val," she chuckled.

"I understand what you meant little sister," said Val as he returned her chuckle.

"I believe it's time to get you back to the hospital Sergeant Barto," the Judge said, "before they think that I've kidnapped you."

"We'll head out this way," he told his family, "and he can let us know in a couple days when everything sinks in."

Mrs. Waltman came over and hugged Barto and said, "You're always welcome here Mr. Barto, but I'm afraid you'll have to give up a hug now and again."

"Good night, Mr. Barto," the girls said.

"We hope to see you soon," added Sarah.

This time, the hug from Mrs. Waltman was returned by Barto. He had bonded with this family so quickly. Was he crazy to think he could fit in here and feel at home? The Judge and the entire Waltman family were offering to help him out, and Barto wasn't used to that.

Back at the hospital that night, Barto slept well, even though his mind was racing with numerous hesitations and possibilities.

Chapter 4

THE HEART POT & BUTTERFLY WINDCHIME

It occurred to Samuel Barto that moving into the Waltman house was out of character for him, but it somehow felt right. When he called Judge Waltman from the hospital, he told him that he would like to give the caretaker position a try and thanked him for the opportunity. He was scheduled to be released from the hospital the next day.

"I'll pick you up tomorrow," the Judge said with excitement. "Your truck is at Mom's house already. I had them take it there when Sheriff Bastian told me it had to be moved from where they found you. You can use that, or you can use the family van to move some of your things out of storage. Wait until I tell the family. They'll be thrilled! They've been calling me practically every hour to see if I've heard from you yet."

As they drove up to his new residence, Barto was still a little nervous. The sight of his truck helped calm down his nerves, and the sight of Mrs. Waltman, practically in a sprint coming out to greet him, made everything seem right so far. She was followed closely by her three daughters. "Thank you for helping us out Mr. Barto. We sure are glad to have you here."

This was a big hug moment, almost taking his breath away, but Barto liked it. He replied to the family in general, "Thank you for having me. I'll try not to let you down."

"Pshaw Mr. Barto," Margaret said. "This is going to be great, and we promise not to be too bothersome. You'll get as much privacy as you want."

Elizabeth added, "Can we help you get moved in Mr. Barto? Val says you have some things in storage, and we could help you with them."

"Thank you, ma'am," Barto answered. "I'm thinking I'll do that gradually, so I don't think I'll need help with that, but I do have a motorcycle in there that I'd like to bring over, if that's okay. I could use a ride over there in a few days so I can drive it back."

"Of course it's okay," said Mrs. Waltman. "Poppy always wanted a motorcycle, but kept putting it off."

Sarah spoke up and said, "Just let me know when you want to go get it. Laura and I are always looking for an excuse to go out for a ride."

The first couple of days after his arrival, Barto stayed busy getting oriented and moving in. True to their word, the Waltmans left him alone while he settled in, but did assure him that they were there and more than willing if he needed any help. They had stocked up the small refrigerator in his room and had it full with plenty of drinks and snacks and sandwich stuff for when he wanted a quick and easy meal in between his chores. Otherwise, his room was already in clean and comfortable condition.

Most of his first days at the Waltmans were spent in Poppy's workshop. Barto's father had left quite a few tools in storage. Those, in addition to what Poppy had left in his shop, made for a nice collection with which he could work. He had a chance to prep the mowers and even change the oil in the Waltman truck. His first landscaping job was to revitalize a flower bed at the front of the house.

Soon after he was somewhat settled in, the Waltmans invited him to dinner with the family. Barto politely accepted and looked forward to a good meal and a chance to thank them again for everything they had provided.

At dinner, Barto was directed to sit at the end of the large rectangular dinner table. He remembered that location as the traditional place of honor or as the place for the head of household. On his right side sat Margaret, then Rasheem, and then Elizabeth. On his left was Sarah, with Laura in the middle, and then Mrs. Waltman. Barto noted that the other end of the table was empty and guessed it may have been where Poppy sat, but he wasn't comfortable enough yet to bring that up.

Over a delicious roast beef dinner, Mrs. Waltman invited Barto to visit and use the "library" anytime he wanted to. "Do you read much Mr. Barto?" she asked.

"Yes ma'am, I like to read a lot," Barto replied. "I started loving books when I was a kid. It was sort of like being transported to my own little world."

"That's why I like video games," Rasheem interjected.

Barto smiled and replied, "I'm sure if they had them when I was growing up, they would've been a big thing for me too."

"It's nice to have another man around the house Mr. Barto," Rasheem answered. "You probably understand things way better than all these girls."

Barto smiled at being the other "man" around the house.

"Well, I like to paint," said Susannah. "I'm not a pro, but I can sit in front of a canvas for hours and forget about the worries of being an old woman."

"Don't listen to her Mr. Barto, she's actually very good," said Margaret. "We'll have to show you some samples around the house. I have a profile she painted of me that I have hanging in my bedroom."

Barto had noticed a portrait painting of each member of the family along the far wall of the dining room and was quite impressed.

"We three girls all play the piano," Elizabeth said, "and Sarah can sing like an angel." Sarah smiled with a slight blush.

"How about Laura?" Barto inquired. "Has she started playing the piano yet?"

Sarah answered while smiling at Laura. "I hope one day she will Mr. Barto. Laura is autistic and is mostly in her own special world, but I don't know what I'd do without her."

Barto knew that Autism was mysterious and affected people in so many different ways. He politely nodded his head in understanding and avoided any awkward prattling by not inquiring further. "I can't say I'm musically inclined, but I do like to make windchimes. Maybe Laura would like to come out to the shop later to see some that I've made."

"I'm sure she would love that Mr. Barto," replied Sarah.

After dinner, Barto headed out to the workshop

while the ladies cleaned up and the kids watched TV. Not too much later, Sarah knocked on the workshop door, and she and Laura walked into the newly organized work area.

"It's been a long time since I've been in here," Sarah said. "I don't think Laura's ever been here. You have it fixed up quite cozy." Sarah handed Barto a white ceramic flower pot with painted hearts and a wilted plant draped over the edge. "I saw what you did with the flower bed, and I thought you could use this pot for a plant in here, to brighten things up even more. I'm afraid it's too late for the plant, but it is a nice pot, if I say so myself. I made if for my father at my first Bible school when I was four years old. He called it his "Heart Pot", and he told me he would keep it in this workshop to help brighten it up. He always made me feel special, but I especially remember the fuss he made over this silly pot. I took it in the house after he died, but it always looked better out here."

"Thank you very much Miss Sarah. I'll take real good care of it," he said as he turned the pot and admired his new gift. He sat the pot down on the workbench and invited them in to the middle of the room. A row of pipes and accessories of all different shapes and sizes hung from the ceiling.

"Look at the pretty windchimes Laura," Sarah pointed. She touched the hanging frog, and then the horse, and then the star, which all rang their particular chimes in harmonious tones. Laura's smile got bigger as she stared up at the pretty noise.

Barto reached over to the workbench and picked up another chime and showed it to Laura. "This is my latest," he said, "my first with a butterfly." Laura reached out and touched the butterfly, and the chime sang its high-pitched song. She looked up at her mom with a big smile and then looked back at the chime, fascinated. Barto handed her the chime, and she gently stroked the collective pieces.

After a bit more chitchat, Sarah said, "Thanks for the demonstration Mr. Barto. We don't want to take up any more of your time, and I should get back in the house to help clean up."

Barto looked at Laura and said, "Maybe Laura could stay out here for a while and play with the windchimes. I'll bring her inside in a little bit."

"Actually," Sarah replied, "it looks like she would love that, if you don't mind. She's a good girl, she'll follow you in." Sarah left the workshop realizing that she would normally feel uncomfortable leaving Laura, but she couldn't help but feel safe around Mr. Barto, and she couldn't remember when she saw Laura smile that big.

Barto pointed to the rocker in the corner and said to his young guest, "They tell me that's your grandmother's rocker if you'd like to sit there and hold the chime." Laura sat rocking contentedly while holding the butterfly chime and occasionally stroking the wooden butterfly sail, which caused the pipes to ring. Barto listened with a smile while he puttered with some loose pipes on the bench against the opposite wall.

"I'm going to call you Mr. B."

These were the first words Barto had heard Laura say, and he was somewhat startled. He turned to face her and nodded, "My last name is Barto, so I guess Mr. B is a good name."

"No, Mr. B stands for Mr. Blue," she replied. "I've seen on TV that being blue means being sad, and I noticed that you seem sad a lot when no one else is looking. Are you sad a lot Mr. B?"

Barto never thought of himself as a particularly sad person. Most people thought that because he was quiet, he must be sad. Of course, given his most recent state of mind, he certainly couldn't consider himself a happy person. "Mr. B's fine I guess," he replied with a smile. "My grandfather used to say that you can call him anything you want to, just don't call him late for supper."

Laura said, "Your windchimes are quite wonderful Mr. B. I especially like this butterfly one."

"Then that one is yours," Barto replied. He took the chime and held it high over his head and told her, "I'll get a hook for it, and we can hang it on the porch tomorrow."

"That would be nice Mr. B, thank you. Do you think it would be okay for me to come back and visit you here? I really like talking."

"Of course it's okay. You're welcome here anytime I'm here, and I'll save your seat for you," he said as he pointed at the rocker.

After a few more minutes, Barto said, "I suppose we should get back inside now."

As they approached the workshop door, Laura noticed the Heart Pot on the workbench and picked it up. "Poor plant," she said as she stroked the withered plant with her fingertips. "I'm sure Mr. B will take care of you, and you'll get better." Barto smiled as she put the pot down, and they headed back to the house with Laura holding his hand.

When they walked into the "Room of Souls", Barto smelled the aroma of freshly brewed coffee and quickly accepted a cup when Elizabeth offered. "Time to get ready for bed Laura," said Sarah as she led her to the stairway. "Thank you, Mr. Barto."

"Good night Little One," said Barto.

As the Judge had pointed out, the kitchen's sitting area was a popular place for evening conversation at the Waltman house. The chairs were comfortable, and the area was warm, almost as if the oven was used as an extra heater. Barto was feeling more and more at home with the company he was now keeping. When Sarah returned from upstairs, they all sat around with their coffee and talked small talk. Sarah bragged to her mother and sisters about Barto's windchimes and how Laura had taken to them.

After his coffee cup was empty, Barto lifted himself out of his chair and announced his intention to retire for the evening. "By the way, I told Laura I would hang her butterfly chime on the porch tomorrow, I hope that's okay?"

"That would be lovely Mr. Barto, thank you," Susannah answered.

As he opened the door to the outside, he said, "I'm going to check on my truck and head down to my room."

"Good night, Mr. Barto," came a chorus from the ladies.

Barto stopped and looked back in with a smile. He said, "You have a great daughter Miss Sarah, and she likes sitting in your chair very much Mrs. Waltman. She kind of surprised me when she started talking about the butterfly windchime," he said and continued with a slight chuckle, "and she said she is going to start calling me Mr. B." He did not explain the real reason for the name, but knew that they could and would relate the B to Barto. "Good night, ladies," he said as he closed the door.

After Barto had shut the door, all four ladies sat stiff and silent in their chairs. Sarah's mouth had fallen open in shock and amazement. Margaret finally broke the silence and asked, "Did he say Laura had talked to him?" All the others said nothing, but slowly nodded their heads. Yes, Barto had specifically said that Laura had talked to him about windchimes and had even announced what her new name for him would be. No one had ever heard Laura say a single word. Not only was Laura autistic, she had always been totally mute.

PART TWO

Chapter 5

LAURA

Sarah was 16 years old when she gave birth to tiny Laura Susannah Waltman. She had decided on "Laura" for her little girl's first name soon after she had learned how to read. Her real-life daughter was named after her favorite character in her favorite children's book. She decided on the middle name "Susannah" after the love and support she hadn't expected from her mother. Susannah Waltman had certainly not approved of her 16 year old daughter's pregnancy, but she and her older daughters accepted it with grace and compassion. Instead of disdain for the teenage unwed mother, they showered their love on Sarah and her child. Sarah and her family accepted Laura's autism right away, and it was hard not to adore the little girl whose pretty face always wore a smile.

On the evening that Barto described his conversation with Laura, Sarah quietly but quickly went to her room where her daughter was still filtering through the picture book she had been provided. "Laura, talk to

41

me sweetie. Tell me about Mr. B's windchimes." Laura looked up at her mom, smiled, and then quickly looked back at her book contentedly. Silly me, Sarah thought. Mr. Barto must've imagined the conversation. When Sarah went back downstairs, all of the other ladies looked at her face for a sign, but when they saw none, they went about their business as usual.

"I think maybe I would've imagined that kind of reaction from Laura too, if I were him," said Elizabeth.

"I can imagine her talking to me all the time, and I haven't even been through what he has lately," said Sarah.

"He's probably on some meds, for pain and maybe other things too," added Margaret.

With her family's help, Sarah's mood had almost recovered from its artificial high and subsequent letdown. However, she did have a hard time falling to sleep that night while she was thinking about what Mr. Barto had said.

The first thing Barto thought of when he woke the next day was the promise he had made to Laura about hanging her butterfly windchime. Morning coffee with Mrs. Waltman was becoming an everyday ritual, and this morning over their first cup, Barto told her that he was going to work on the porch today to get it back in shape. He also reminded her of his promise to Laura about hanging her windchime.

"That sounds good Mr. Barto. The porch has needed some sprucing up for quite a few seasons, and the windchime will be a nice touch. Maybe we could break it in a bit this evening and eat our dinner out there. We're planning on an early meal of roast beef sandwiches before we go over to the Veteran's Center. It's our turn to help serve the evening meal tonight, and the girls sing and play music for the Vets. My girls are very good, and the guys seem to enjoy the entertainment. Why don't you come with us Mr. Barto? We could introduce you to some of your fellow veterans."

"We'll see about that ma'am," Barto replied. "But in any case, I'll have the porch ready for this evening." Barto was pretty sure he wasn't going to go to the Vet Center, tonight or any other night. The thought of interacting with his fellow veterans was actually quite appealing, but his personality was not proactive, and he was uncomfortable when trying to start conversations and interactions with people he had never met.

After his morning coffee meeting with Mrs. Waltman, Barto wandered over to the workshop to pick up his tools and supplies to get the porch back in shape. When he opened the door to the workshop, he immediately noticed the Heart Pot he had left on the workbench last evening. The formerly wilted and lifeless plant in Sarah's gift was now flourishing with color and life. He looked closer and confirmed that the plant was the same variety as the one Sarah had given to him last night. Apparently, Sarah had changed her mind and had gone out and bought a new plant to replace the old wilted one. It was quite impressive and did indeed lend a homey feel to the workshop.

After retrieving his needed tools and the butterfly windchime, Barto set out to upgrade the porch area. He secured all of the loose boards, scraped away the loose paint and debris, and prepared several hanging planters and landscaping beds surrounding the porch. After a trip to the hardware store for paint and landscaping materials, he resurfaced the wood with a fresh coat of paint and filled the hanging pots and border with plants and flowers. Even though he couldn't find the same plant as the one Sarah had bought for his workshop, he was satisfied with the overall results. He cleaned and tightened the lawn furniture, and the project was complete when he hung Laura's butterfly chime in the middle of the trellis that made up the roof over half of the porch. The slight breeze was perfect to help dry the paint and produce a pleasant high-pitched sound from the newly hung chime.

All of the Waltman women were impressed with the newly refurbished porch, and it made the early evening meal that much more enjoyable. "Would you like to come along with us tonight Mr. Barto?" asked Susannah.

Barto hesitated, but politely answered, "Thank you ma'am, but I don't think so. I don't think I'm ready for that yet." He wasn't sure exactly what "yet" meant, but she seemed to accept its meaning. "I think I'll work on some more windchimes this evening. Laura, maybe one day I can show you how to make one." Laura was sitting at the picnic table with her never-ending smile as she finished her potato chips. Although Barto had addressed the statement to her, Laura did not reply and did not seem to notice him speak. "What do you think about that Laura?" he asked.

Laura's attention was still unchanged and even Rasheem noticed Barto's awkward expectation. He said, "She can't talk Mr. Barto."

Sarah picked up on Barto's confused face and said, "Mr. Barto, I mentioned before that Laura was autistic, but I didn't mention that she has never spoken a word. She is mute."

Barto absorbed this information as best as he could while considering his conversations with Laura the night before. "But we talked last night ma'am. We talked about windchimes and she said she was going to call me Mr. B," he said.

"I understand Mr. Barto," Sarah replied. "I often imagine hearing her talk to me too. Perhaps the medicine and your recent experiences have increased your imagination."

Barto was sure he'd heard Laura talk, and he clearly remembered their conversation, but as his mind gathered and focused all the information, he understood that it must be impossible, and he quickly became embarrassed. "I'm sorry ma'am," he said, "you're probably right. You must think I'm crazier now than ever before."

"Not at all Mr. Barto," Sarah replied. "I've always hoped that a miracle would allow Laura to come out of her world into ours, and maybe one day it will."

Barto appreciated the polite manner in which Sarah had handled his embarrassment, but he needed to leave and break the spell. "Thank you again for the meal," he spoke aloud to no one in particular. "I guess I'll get started on some of my windchimes now."

After Barto disappeared into the workshop, the ladies started cleaning up, and Sarah spoke up, "You know, I wonder if Mr. Barto would mind if Laura stayed with him in his shop with the windchimes while we're gone. We won't be gone very long, and she wouldn't be a bother."

Margaret spoke up, "Don't get too excited Sarah. Laura is a sweetie, but she is what she is for many years now." Laura sat quietly staring up at the motions and sounds of her windchime.

"Don't be silly Margaret. I have no expectations, but she sure does love those chimes. What do you think Laura? Would you like to stay with Mr. B?" She held out her hand, and Laura instinctively grabbed her and followed her to the workshop.

Sarah knocked on Barto's workshop door and when she entered, she noticed that Barto was measuring some pipes that were next to be cut. "Mr. Barto, I don't want to put you on the spot, but I thought that maybe you could use some company while we were at the Veteran's Center, and Laura sure does love your windchimes."

"Of course," answered Barto without hesitation. "Even if we can't talk, we share a love for these chimes."

"She'll sit for hours and watch the chimes if you let her, and she's always a very good girl."

"I would like her company a lot ma'am," he answered truthfully. "We'll be fine."

As Sarah was leaving, Barto remembered, "Oh, I almost forgot, thank you for the new plant ma'am. You didn't have to get me a new one," as he pointed towards the flourishing plant in the pretty Heart Pot.

Sarah looked over at the Heart Pot and saw the impressive plant embedded inside. "That is quite a nice plant Mr. Barto, but it's not from me. I will take credit for that very attractive pot though." She smiled brightly and headed out the door.

After Sarah was gone, Barto led Laura to her grandmother's chair and handed her a chime with a rocking horse figure at the bottom.

"Hmmm," Barto exhaled as he stared at the flourishing plant. "I wonder who would have replaced the plant then," he said out loud to no one.

"It is quite a nice plant," sounded a voice behind him. Barto quickly turned to see Laura staring intently at the rocking horse chime. He made a mental note to get back to the doctor very soon and ask him about decreasing his medication dosage before he went totally out of his mind. Shaking his head, he went back to the workbench and resumed his measurements of the pipes.

"Why does the rocking horse windchime sound different than the butterfly windchime?" Laura asked.

Barto dropped the pipes on the cement floor causing a loud clanging noise. He spun towards Laura and noticed her staring at him with a smile. Mechanically, Barto replied to the Laura Hallucination, "The longer the pipe, the lower the pitch. The shorter pipes have a higher pitch."

"Well I like them both," replied the Laura Hallucination. She rocked out of the chair and retrieved the errant pipes that Barto had dropped. "And this one will be a lower pitch because it is longer, right?"

"That's right," Barto said. After his initial surprise and confusion, he simply accepted that he was hallucinating and figured he would go with it until he could get his medicine dosage reduced.

"Mr. B, do you really think you could teach me how to make a windchime one day?"

"Of course," he replied as he stared at the Laura Hallucination. He had always dreamed about showing his granddaughter how to make one. "The hardest part is the sail, that piece on the bottom that looks like a rocking horse and catches the wind. It can be tough cutting some shapes."

"Well I like this rocking horse," she said. "But I really like my butterfly chime."

Barto knew that he was basically talking to himself, but the Laura Hallucination was very realistic and pleasant to talk to; very good meds indeed he thought. "I was told you didn't talk much," Barto said. "How is it you talk to me and not to anyone else?"

"I don't know Mr. B," she answered. "Most of the time it seems like I'm in a dream world where I can't talk and I can't see and I can't hear things very clearly either. And then when Mommy left me here last night and today, everything cleared up. I can talk, and I can see what I want to see, and I can hear you, and I can understand. It's like I've stepped out of my dream."

Barto couldn't help but be entranced by this enthusiastic little girl and her story, even though he knew she wasn't real. "Do you remember anything around you when you're in your dream?"

"Only a little bit," she replied with a smile. "I remember being alone with Aunt Elizabeth once and she kept trying to get me to call her "Aunt Lizzie". She kept saying, call me Aunt Lizzie sweetie, just call me Aunt Lizzie."

"And then when I was alone with Aunt Margaret, she said the same kind of thing except she kept saying, call me "Aunt Maggie" Laura, please say Aunt Maggie." The Laura Hallucination looked down at her hands a bit sadly and continued, "I tried Mr. B, I tried really hard, but I just couldn't talk back to them."

"I know you did and so do they. It's not your fault Little One."

The Laura Hallucination perked back up and said, "I've heard Grandma talk about miracles, and she said that maybe one day there will be a miracle that could make me talk and come out of my own special world."

Barto listened intently, almost forgetting that this conversation was all a figment of his imagination. If it was a hallucination or a dream, he didn't want it to end.

"Maybe you're my "Nudge" Mr. B. I heard Mommy say that maybe God nudges people every once in a while, and it sometimes looks like a miracle. I don't understand it fully, but maybe God nudged you to come and help me. That would be sort of a miracle wouldn't it Mr. B?"

"I don't know about that Laura. I can't imagine myself being part of a miracle or being a Nudge." Her statements made Barto uncomfortable so he tried to deflect her attention. "I do know that I'm hungry for dessert, and your grandmother made a blueberry pie earlier. How about we get some pie and wash it down with a big glass of milk?" he said hopefully.

With a big smile, Laura nodded in agreement. As they walked towards the house, Barto noticed that Laura seemed to look around and up and down as if she was trying to absorb the view from out of her dream; strange actions from a hallucination he thought.

They both had an excellent piece of pie and washed it down with a glass of cold milk. After their treat, Barto suggested that they watch some TV in the greatroom. The conversation from the Laura Hallucination was less serious than before and centered on what was going on during the TV show. When Laura abruptly stopped talking, Barto looked over at her to see what was wrong. At the same time, he could hear the Waltman family come into the house and make their way to the greatroom.

"There you are," said a smiling Sarah. "Is there anything good on the TV?"

Barto looked over at Laura, who was now staring at the TV with her normal smile, and looked back at Sarah. "Not anymore I guess," he replied, "but Laura and I had a very nice evening. We had a piece of your wonderful pie Mrs. Waltman, I hope that was okay."

"That's what it's there for Mr. Barto, I hope you liked it."

"It was delicious ma'am, and I'm sure Laura liked it too."

"Thank you for letting Laura stay with you Mr. Barto," Sarah said. "I think you've found a new best friend. She seems quite taken with you."

"My pleasure ma'am, her company is welcome anytime. We had a nice conversation," he said in a way that everyone knew he was joking on himself. "I guess it's time to get downstairs for the night. Tomorrow I would like to work on the lawn."

"Sounds good Mr. Barto, we sure are glad you're here to help us out," said Susannah.

"By the way," said Barto as he walked towards the basement door. "Thank you to whoever bought me the plant for the workshop. It looks great in Miss Sarah's Heart Pot."

All the ladies looked at each other, shaking their heads in amusement. Margaret spoke for all of them and said, "It wasn't any of us Mr. Barto; maybe you have a secret admirer."

"Hah, maybe." Barto laughed and added as he headed down the stairs, "Good night ladies."

Chapter 6

NUDGES & MIRACLES

Several nights after talking to the Laura Hallucination, Barto found himself relaxing with the Waltmans on the porch, sharing light conversation. Both Rasheem and Laura were already settling in upstairs, and Susannah had provided the customary coffee and pie. Barto had begun to look forward to these pleasant gatherings and informal conversation while in the company of the Waltman women.

"You really must come with us to the Veteran's Center one evening Mr. Barto," Susannah said. "There are some great guys there, and I'm sure you would feel right at home."

"Poppy made quite a few friends there too," Margaret added.

Elizabeth spoke up, "Most of the guys just like the company of their fellow veterans. They play cards and shoot what pool they can on that one beat up table. And they throw darts, watch TV, and come around for a good meal now and then. I just wish there was a better place for them. The building is an old warehouse, and the furnishings are worn out hand-me-downs from other Vet Centers and area offices. We've been trying to get better government support, but even though the need keeps growing, we can't seem to get anywhere."

"But still, I'm sure the guys have been in a lot worse conditions," said Susannah. "None of the Vets ever complain, and we do fix some good meals for them. Of course, the highlight of their evening is when my girls give them some musical entertainment."

"There are some of the guys that come for help too," said Margaret as she looked directly at Barto. "A few of our volunteers try to link them up with the resources they need and the help they've earned."

Barto felt uncomfortable as he noticed that Margaret was looking at him when she made her last statement.

Susannah noticed Barto's discomfort and changed the subject of their conversation. "Mr. Barto, I noticed you rode your motorcycle last Sunday. Were you on your way to church?"

"No ma'am," Barto replied, "at least not the way most people think of Sunday church. It's a bit complicated, but I'll try and explain." Barto settled into his chair a bit and began. "There is a church in White Deer Valley that's over 100 years old. My great-great-great grandfather settled there and was one of its first members back in the 1840s. Around 1900, the congregation decided they needed more space, so they built a new church on the same spot. That's the one that's there now." Barto looked down at his hands and added, "That's where they found me before I met you."

The Waltmans remained politely silent and

attentive while waiting for Barto to continue his story. He straightened back up in his chair and continued.

"In the 1940s, the government took over the land in that area and ran all the people off. They built some prisons on the land, and they used the church and kept up the cemetery. Eventually, the prison expanded and moved down the road. Even though they still own the land, the church is abandoned. At least they do still take care of it. I go up there every Sunday if I can, and even though the church is locked, I sit there and enjoy the quiet and imagine what it must have been like 100 years ago. I guess you could say that I go there when I need my soul recharged. I thought maybe one day I would make some windchimes and hang them near the church and cemetery."

Susannah nodded her head in understanding. "Sounds to me like you go to your church for the same reason most people go to theirs. I'd like to visit your church one day Mr. Barto."

"I'll be right back," Barto said as he got up from his chair. After a quick trip into the workshop, Barto reappeared with a windchime in his hand. "I installed a hook earlier," he said as he hung the windchime several feet from Laura's butterfly chime. The new windchime sported pipes that were slightly longer than hers and the sail was a helicopter. He had wood burned "POPPY" onto both sides of the sail. Soon after it was hung, it began to harmonize with the smaller butterfly chime.

When Susannah saw the detail and the engraving, she rose from her chair and gave Barto a huge hug. "Thank you Mr. Barto. I'll certainly never forget Poppy, but forgive me if I smile just a little bit more every time I hear that chime."

After they had sat back down, Barto chuckled a

53

bit while he was looking up at the chimes, and Sarah noticed. "What's funny Mr. Barto?" she asked.

"I was just thinking about a few nights back when Laura and I were in the workshop, and we talked," he laughed. "Let me assure you that the doctors have reduced my meds since then, but that night we talked more about windchimes."

The Waltmans appreciated his humor and smiled. "What did you talk about Mr. Barto?" Margaret asked.

Barto felt only slightly embarrassed when she asked about his hallucination. He knew they understood and didn't think any less of him, especially now that his meds had been adjusted. "We talked about windchimes a lot, and she really likes the butterfly chime. We talked about her TV shows too," said Barto as he smiled while looking at Laura's chime swinging in the breeze. "Oh, and she also talked about you ma'am."

"Me?" said Margaret as she scooted up in her chair.

"Yes ma'am. She said that you talked to her when you two were alone. She said you kept asking her to talk; to call you "Aunt Maggie". She said you told her, talk to me sweetie, call me Aunt Maggie."

In the shadows where she was seated, no one noticed Margaret's face when it turned white with shock as their attention was now turned towards Elizabeth when she asked with a smile, "How about me Mr. Barto? Did she say anything about her favorite Aunt?"

Barto smiled and answered, "Well, yes she did as a matter of fact ma'am." He was now getting a lot of enjoyment out of this imagination game. "It was a lot like what she said to her Aunt Maggie. She said when you were alone with her you kept asking her to call you "Aunt Lizzie". Laura, call me Aunt Lizzie she said."

Elizabeth turned the same shade of white as Margaret, and this time everyone noticed the sisters' discomfort. "I'm sorry ma'am," said Barto. "I didn't mean to upset you. I'll stop."

Brushing the apology aside, Margaret said, "Elizabeth and I hate those names Mr. Barto, but we both have a friendly bet on who Laura would talk to first. Those are the names we agreed on that we would get her to say."

Elizabeth added, "No one knew about that but us, not even Sarah. We did talk to Laura, and we asked her to call us those names. We just wanted to see if one of her aunts could produce a miracle and get her to speak."

Laura's aunts were still in shock and they had no more words. Everyone was a bit more attentive now, and the mood was a lot more serious. Susannah looked away from her daughters and asked, "Did she say anything else Mr. Barto?"

Barto was hesitant to answer. He wasn't sure he understood everything that they said, but he knew he couldn't stop now. The Waltmans would not let him.

Apprehensively, he answered, "She talked about you too ma'am. She said she heard her grandma and her mommy talking once." He paused to gather his thoughts and clarify his memory. "She said that you talked about miracles and how one day a miracle might happen to her, and she might talk and come out of her own special world. And you too Miss Sarah. She said something I didn't really understand, but I think I remember. Laura said that you talked about God sometimes and how he helped guide people, and sometimes it seemed like miracles." Barto tried a smile to break up the mood and continued, "My meds must've really kicked in because she said you called that a nudge. She even suggested that I might be her Nudge to help her…"

When she heard Barto say the word nudge, Sarah gasped and dropped her coffee mug, shattering it on the concrete floor. Barto noticed the shock on all of the Waltmans' faces, and he was sure he was the cause. He stuttered, "I'm sorry ma'am… my meds…"

Margaret cut him off and said, "Mr. Barto, it's not your meds. Only Elizabeth and I knew what we had said to Laura, just as you… just as she had described."

"And the conversation about being nudged," added Sarah. "We don't talk about that to anyone else, just us, but Laura is around sometimes too."

"It's not your meds Mr. Barto," Margaret repeated. "It apparently never was. Laura is talking to you."

Barto sat silent, not knowing how to react or what to say. After several moments of mutual silence, Barto asked, "What did she mean by nudged?"

Susannah squirmed in her chair, sat up a little bit and leaned forward. "Are you a religious man Mr. Barto?"

"I'm not exactly sure ma'am," Barto replied. "I do believe we have a Creator. I'm just not sure if he is named God or Allah or whatever his name is, and I don't know whether he is Jewish or Christian or Muslim or something else. I am pretty sure we didn't evolve from some microbe a billion years ago unless that is what the Creator wanted. Someone once called me a Deist, but I don't know exactly what that means."

"You are right Mr. Barto," Susannah said. "Laura did hear me talk about miracles, because I believe that my God is all-powerful and therefore he has the power to do anything. I believe in the power of prayer, and I pray every day for a miracle for my granddaughter."

Margaret said, "Mr. Barto, a Deist believes in a Creator who created everything and then stepped back to let everything happen as it may. No miracles, no divine intervention. He basically lets everything happen without His help at all."

Sarah spoke up, "My sisters and I pray too Mr. Barto, but not exactly for the same reasons that our mother does. We don't pray to our Creator when we need something or when someone we know needs help. We trust Him to know what's best, even if we don't understand why sometimes. We pray as a way to maintain an intimacy with our Creator. We pray to Him because we know that we always have someone to count on that cares about us and who will always be there to listen."

Elizabeth said, "I believe He gave us free will and the choices we make allow us to succeed gloriously or fail miserably. Sometimes things go our way and sometimes they don't. Maybe that was our Creator's plan; to have us experience all the ups and downs of life. I think we all must be here for a purpose. Maybe to learn or gain experience, and maybe that purpose is unique for everyone."

Margaret added, "But I can't believe that a Creator so wonderful and as powerful as ours would just step aside without lending a hand every once in awhile. We are all His children after all, and what parent wouldn't step in once in awhile with a helping hand. We call that a nudge."

Susannah said, "Laura heard me when I suggested that miracles might be God's way of helping us out once in a while. He created us all Mr. Barto, no matter what religion or lack of faith that we may have. And every once in awhile, maybe He gives us a nudge to help us along."

Sarah said, "Sometimes a nudge might be loud and obvious, and other times we may not even know we've been nudged, and no one around us notices either."

Barto understood what they were saying, but he was having a hard time digesting the information, especially since Laura had suggested that he was her Nudge. "I'm just not sure. It's hard for me to believe that I could be any part of that."

Susannah smiled and replied, "Maybe you're not part of anything special Mr. Barto. Maybe you just happened along at the right time, and maybe Laura will never talk to you or anyone else ever again. But maybe you *WERE* nudged here to help Laura and us out. Some things are true whether you believe them or not."

Sarah said excitedly, "And wouldn't it be wonderful if God nudged you in our direction and then maybe stepped back to see what would happen? Wouldn't it be wonderful if you are Laura's Nudge Mr. B?"

Barto noticed that Sarah had borrowed Laura's name for him and took that as a sign that she now wanted to believe that Laura actually did talk to him; maybe even more than he believed it himself.

"Do you think it would be okay if Laura could spend some more time with you in the workshop; maybe tomorrow night?" Sarah asked somewhat excitedly.

"I suppose so Miss Sarah, but I'm not so sure I would get your hopes up."

Barto's thoughts went back to the cemetery and beyond. Could it have been a coincidence that his father wasn't killed in one of his three wars, or his father's father in his war, or his other ancestors in theirs? One bullet could have ended the line, and he may never have existed. Or what about the Sheriff finding him before he bled to death, or being assigned a judge who needed a caretaker to help out his family… and a little autistic girl who apparently can only speak and come out of her dream world when she is alone with him?

Were these coincidences or some of life's cruel jokes? He had said to Sarah, "I'm not so sure I would get my hopes up." Barto now wondered who he actually meant for that warning.

Chapter 7

WINDOW GAZING

The next morning, Barto walked upstairs for his regular cup of coffee, and all four Waltman ladies and Laura were sitting on the kitchen dinette benches. When he walked in, he was greeted with a chorus of good mornings and other pleasantries, and he noticed them all looking at Laura for any reaction at his arrival.

"Good morning ladies," answered Barto. "And good morning to you Laura," he said.

All the ladies again looked expectantly at Laura, but she seemed not to notice his presence and continued eating her cereal. It was apparent now that if Laura could talk to Barto, it would not be when the other Waltmans were present. Barto still had his doubts. Everything had happened so quickly, he still was not sure what would happen when Laura and he were alone tonight as promised. Sarah, on the other hand, was animated with excitement, and she was sure that Mr. B and Laura would talk some more this evening.

Barto's entire day involved mowing the large yard, edging the sidewalks, and trimming the bushes. It took him the entire day, but when he had cleaned and put away his tools, he still had enough time to shower and put on clean clothes before dinner. The evening meal itself seemed special that night, and Barto enjoyed the food and the conversation. Nothing was spoken of the upcoming appointment between Barto and Laura, but everyone had it at the foremost of their minds, even though they small-talked about the weather and the smells of flowers and freshly cut grass.

When Barto announced that it was time for him to head out to the workshop, he simply looked at Laura and then at Sarah.

"We'll be out shortly if that's okay Mr. B," said Sarah.

"That's fine ma'am," he replied rather nervously.

Several moments later, when Sarah told her mother and sisters that she was going to take Laura out to the workshop, they simply nodded their heads in agreement. They were not going to allow themselves the luxury of expectation until they knew for sure that the nudge was real. On the other hand, Sarah was practically giddy with anticipation. She understood that she was setting herself up for the ultimate joy or the ultimate heartache, and her mother and sisters knew that too. They wanted to stay rational in case Sarah needed them.

Sarah led Laura to the workshop, knocked on the door, and led her to Susannah's rocking chair. Her only words before she left were, "Thank you Mr. B."

"I'll bring her in later Miss Sarah," Barto answered, and Sarah left in a hurry. Barto wasn't really sure how to begin the encounter, so he simply went back to work on drawing the outlines for more of the sails he would cut out of a six-inch wide wooden board. When Laura didn't speak and simply rocked in the rocking chair, Barto inwardly started to panic. What if it all was really a dream? What if he had been talking to a hallucination after all? How could he face the family if it turned out he wasn't really Laura's Nudge?

Hopefully, he said to Laura, "That plant sure is doing well now don't you think Laura?" as he pointed at the plant in the Heart Pot.

Laura glanced at the plant and then at Barto and replied, "It certainly is a nice plant Mr. B."

Barto had never been more relieved than when he heard Laura's voice, especially when he heard her call him Mr. B. He definitely wanted to keep the conversation's momentum going. "You know, it was in bad shape when your mom gave it to me, but soon after you held it, it turned back into this flourishing plant. Do you think you had something to do with that?"

"I did talk to it a little, maybe that helped," she replied with a giggle. "Thank you for helping me talk again Mr. B. I feel so different when I'm here with you. Everything is so much clearer."

"Laura, do you remember anything since we were here last?"

"I'm sorry Mr. B," she said softly, "I guess I went back into my dream world."

Barto grabbed his stool and dragged it closer to Laura and looked directly into her eyes. "When I talked to you last, I didn't think you were real. I thought maybe I was in my own dream world."

Laura smiled back at Barto's big grin.

"But you are real aren't you Little One?"

"I sure feel real Mr. B, and so does the plant and this hammer and this chair too." Laura stood up and started wandering about and chattered about everything she touched as she absorbed the wonder of her new and clearer world. She stopped talking when she reached the side window that overlooked the road and the passing cars. "Do you suppose we could go out there one day Mr. B? Maybe I could see things more clearly out there in my new world."

"We could try, but to be honest, I'm not sure what would happen. This is all still a mystery to me, and I'll have to ask your mom's permission of course." He hesitated and added, "I'm not exactly sure if you'll be in a dream world or a clear world, but it might be worth a try."

She turned towards Barto and said, "You ARE my Nudge aren't you Mr. B? It's you that brings me out of my dream world. I know that for sure now."

"I'm not sure what to say about that Little One, but it might be interesting to see how this plays out. Your family is very anxious to hear everything about our visit today, especially your mommy."

Laura looked down sadly, and with tears forming in her eyes she said, "Mommy must be so disappointed in me Mr. B. I've tried to talk to her, I really have, but... I just can't. I've wanted to tell her that I love her very much and how much I like it when she sings to me in bed before I go to sleep. Will you tell her I especially like it when she sings the Baby Dumbo song to me? She can sing like an angel Mr. B," she said a bit more brightly.

"So I've heard," replied Barto as he returned her smile.

"I've seen on TV that when people were bad when they were young, they would be punished when they got older. I was thinking that maybe she was a bad little girl when she was growing up," she said looking down at her hands sadly. "And maybe I'm her punishment. She must be very disappointed that she has me for her daughter."

"I know that's not true Laura," he quickly interjected. "And maybe you talking to me is just the beginning; at least I hope so," he said with a smile as he attempted to cheer up the little girl.

For the rest of the evening, Laura talked about anything and everything that came to her mind, and Barto was genuinely interested in what she had to say. He wanted to absorb as much as possible so that he could tell the Waltmans and share Laura's joy of her new world. He knew by how she spoke that many of her conversational subjects were from the TV she watched. He suspected that she also absorbed a lot when she was around her family, even if she didn't remember their encounters.

Laura looked back out the window and smiled in anticipation. She glanced down and noticed a lifeless Monarch butterfly on the windowsill. When she touched it, she let out an "Ooooo" and quickly jerked her hand back. Barto smiled when he saw the dead butterfly and thought about little girls and their normal reactions to bugs. But Laura surprised Barto when she slowly reached down and carefully picked up the butterfly and held it in her outstretched palms.

"I should've cleaned the window areas better," Barto said.

"Oh no Mr. B, it's beautiful. Just like my windchime."

Barto nodded his head in agreement and then watched in amazement as the butterfly started flapping its wings into a straight up position in Laura's palm. After several more soft flaps while nestled in her hands, the butterfly took off and started flying all over the room.

Laura smiled hugely and glanced at Mr. B and then back at the butterfly as she followed it while skipping around the room.

Barto's gaze, on the other hand, was filled with amazement as he followed the butterfly's flight around the workshop. He now wondered what exactly he had gotten himself into and whether or not he HAD been nudged to come here.

When the time finally came to go back to the house, Laura didn't seem as disappointed as Barto had anticipated. She said "Thank you Mr. B, do you think we can talk again soon?"

Barto smiled large and replied, "You can count on that Little One, maybe tomorrow night?"

Laura took Mr. B's hand, and they walked towards the house. Soon after the lights went out in the workshop and the door was closed and secure, the forgotten Monarch butterfly finished its flight and landed on the plant in the Heart Pot, safe and secure for the night.

Chapter 8

A VERY GOOD GIRL

When Laura and Mr. B entered the Waltman house, all the ladies were stationed in the kitchen sitting room. All four of them looked up immediately from their books and magazines and searched Barto's face for any sign of what had transpired in the workshop. Barto quickly noticed their attention and captured Sarah's eyes. His smile and slight up-and-down nod confirmed what Sarah had been hoping and praying for in the last 24 hours. She bolted out of her chair and reached for Laura's hand and said, "Time to get ready for bed Laura. Did you have a good time with Mr. B?"

Laura held her mother's hand and walked passively with her to the upwards stairwell. Sarah called back to the group in the kitchen, "I'll be right back."

Barto and the remaining ladies seemed to silently agree that they would wait until Sarah returned before the conversation would return to Laura in the workshop. Susannah busied herself with coffee for the group while

Margaret and Elizabeth continued to compliment Barto on his afternoon landscaping work. Barto settled into his unofficially assigned chair and enjoyed his coffee along with a couple of homemade chocolate chip cookies that Susannah had snuck onto a small plate and offered to Barto along with his brew. Other than a responding "Thank You" a few times, he was reserving his conversation for when Sarah returned.

When Sarah reentered the kitchen, she grabbed the cup of coffee that was offered to her by her mother's outstretched hand and headed directly to her chair. She had barely sat down when she said, "How was Laura tonight Mr. B?"

Barto took notice that all of the Waltman sisters had taken to addressing him as Mr. B, Laura's name for him. They now seemed convinced that Laura was actually talking to him. "She was quite talkative Miss Sarah," he answered as Sarah smiled a big Laura smile. "We talked about windchimes of course and about the TV shows that she watches. I think maybe she gets a lot of her information from the TV, and I also think she absorbs some things when she is around you ladies, but she doesn't remember that as much." Barto paused to gather everything he could remember about their conversation.

"When she was looking out the window, she asked me if we could go outside one day when she wasn't in her dream world. She wants to see out there when her mind is clear. I told her I couldn't guarantee what might happen if we left the house area, but if it was okay with you…"

Sarah didn't hesitate and interrupted, "Of course Mr. B, if it works out for you. Maybe she could ride with you to the hardware store or the like."

Barto nodded and continued, "We both talked

about why she can talk when we're alone together and not when someone else is around, but we didn't have a good answer." Barto was hoping the ladies would have some input and some wise interpretation, but they all seemed just as mystified.

Margaret said, "Well maybe we'll learn more as time goes by, but right now it's exciting that she can talk, even if only to you."

Barto didn't want to quell the upbeat mood, but he remembered more of his conversation with Laura. "Miss Sarah, she thinks that you might be disappointed in her and maybe you wish she wasn't your daughter. She said that she saw something on TV that suggested that you might have been a bad girl growing up and that she was your punishment."

Before Sarah could answer, Susannah spoke up. "Mr. Barto, I've been blessed with four of the best children anyone could ever ask for. When Poppy died…" she hesitated and then continued, "I don't think I would've made it without them. And even now… they've always been my reason to live, and they always will be." She looked Barto intently into his eyes and said, "Mr. Barto, you tell my granddaughter, Sarah was most definitely not a bad girl when she was growing up."

Sarah settled into her chair a bit and said, "I was 16 when I became pregnant with Laura and of course, I wasn't married. Her father wanted nothing to do with us. He moved away, and I've never heard from him since. At first that bothered me, but with my family's support, I realize we're just fine. I went to church every Sunday before that, but after Laura was born, I became a loose teenager in their eyes. I'm sure there are a lot of those people that would tell you that she *IS* my punishment, but I know that's not true. A punishment would never give me as much joy as Laura does."

"In fact, what Mom said must be true. I've been blessed with the greatest gift I could have ever asked for. I must have been a very good girl." Sarah leaned forward in her chair and said to Barto, "Will you make sure you tell her that Mr. Barto?"

"Yes ma'am, I will," he replied with a broad smile.

After a few more sips of coffee and a pause to absorb Mr. B's information, Sarah sat back up and asked, "What does she sound like Mr. B?"

"Ma'am?" he replied confused.

"When I held her as a baby, I would think and wonder what her voice would sound like. I know it's silly, but even when she grew older, and we found out she couldn't speak, I would always try to imagine what her voice would sound like."

"That's not silly Miss Sarah," he replied. "Her voice is lovely. I haven't been around little girls very much, but I enjoy hearing her talk. She talks so calmly, but her energy is infectious." Sarah seemed content and she settled back into her chair with a satisfied smile.

"I've always wondered what kind of voice my son has now as an adult," Barto announced thoughtfully.

"You have a son Mr. B?" Elizabeth asked excitedly.

Barto smiled politely but then looked down and stared at his shoes. "His name is Adam, and he probably doesn't even know I exist. When I was young, my girlfriend's parents hated me, so we eloped. I joined the Army soon after that so I could get us away from them and maybe make something of myself. A couple years after that, we had Adam." Because Sarah had opened up her experiences with him, he felt obligated to continue as the ladies sat quietly and patiently.

"When I was sent to Desert Storm, my wife felt like it would be better if she and Adam went and lived with her parents while I was gone. When the Army first told me I was going to be deployed, they sent me home for a couple of hours to get a few more things packed. I remember wanting to stop at Adam's daycare center, but I just passed right by on my way to catch the plane. I didn't even say goodbye to him. I just couldn't do it. I didn't know how to tell my four-year-old son that I was going to war. I thought about that the whole time I was there, and I've thought about it ever since." Barto paused and then continued. "While I was gone, my in-laws convinced my wife that I was no good, and she wrote me that she wanted a divorce."

Margaret spoke up and said, "It's amazing to me, but the divorce and split-up rate goes way up when a loved one is deployed like that."

Barto appreciated the breather from his story, but then he continued. "I haven't talked to him since then. They made me promise not to and said it would be best for him."

"Why not talk to him now Mr. B?" Elizabeth asked.

"No Miss Elizabeth, it's been too long now, he probably hates me anyway. Every time I've visited around here, I would check up on him, but I wouldn't want to disrupt his life. He's a teacher," Barto said proudly. "He's married and has a little girl. Her name is Rebecca."

"You're a grandfather Mr. B!" said Susannah excitedly.

Barto half-smiled and nodded in agreement.

The Waltmans didn't feel comfortable asking any more about Barto's son, and Barto was content to end the subject right there. "Miss Sarah, I almost forgot to tell you something else Laura said to me. She says that you sing to her at bedtime and that you can sing like an angel."

Sarah smiled brightly and said, "I didn't know if she could hear me or not."

"She does ma'am, and she said she really likes it when you sing the baby song from *Dumbo*."

"She does hear me," Sarah beamed as she rose from her chair and put her hand on Barto's arm. "Thank you so much for giving me more of my daughter Mr. B, but if you'll excuse me, I think I'll see if Laura is still awake. Maybe she would like a good night song."

PART THREE

Chapter 9

THE VETERAN'S CENTER

Several months had passed since Sergeant Barto had started living with the Waltmans, and over that time, the Waltmans had often asked him if he would like to accompany them on their trip to the Veteran's Center.

Over their morning coffee, Barto listened to Susannah and Margaret as they were talking about their current involvement at the Vet Center. Today was the Waltmans' turn to serve the meal and provide the entertainment. Additionally, Margaret was in charge of picking up some cases of provisions from the local food bank. Because of a changed appointment with one of the veterans who she helped, Margaret asked Barto if he would pick up the supplies and drop them off at the Center's kitchen.

"I don't formally counsel the Vets anymore Mr. Barto, but I like to help them find someone that will."

"You used to be a counselor Miss Margaret?" Barto asked. "I bet you were a good one, but why don't you counsel anymore?"

With her shoulders back and her head proudly up, she replied firmly, "I was once married to a police officer Mr. Barto." Her voice faded quickly, and her gaze drifted to the floor when she added, "He was killed in the line of duty a few years back, and I had a rough time with that. My family found my stash of pills before I could use them to end my life."

"I'm so very sorry Miss Margaret," Barto said.

"You see Mr. Barto, I also knew what it was like to think I had no reason to live, but my family came through for me again. But since that time, I haven't felt comfortable counseling others on their depression and the choices they can make to solve their illness. I still want to help, so I try and put them in touch with those people who can assist them. Some of them are the same people that helped me."

Barto agreed to pick up the supplies, and he took Laura along for some company. He and Laura had become regular companions over the last few months. She looked forward to the opportunities to come out of her dream world when she was alone with Mr. B, and Barto enjoyed the energy of the little girl.

After picking up several cases of food, Barto was shown where to put the boxes inside the kitchen. Once inside, Susannah suggested that he stay and listen to her daughters as they entertained the Vets. Although he was apprehensive about staying, he did want to hear the Waltman sisters sing and play their music. Sarah had already led Laura to the worn out sofa in front of the smallish TV. Barto joined her on the couch, but knew that she would remain silent as long as there were others around.

Most everyone else was taking advantage of the

meal being served by the Waltmans, but one man, looking about 10 years Barto's elder, stayed in his chair next to the couch in front of the TV. "Looks like it's dinner time," Barto said to him politely.

"Thanks, but I'm not very hungry tonight. I just stopped by for the entertainment."

"Sergeant Samuel Barto," Barto held out his hand to the man.

"Corporal John Shaffer, U.S. Army, Vietnam," the man replied while accepting Barto's handshake.

"You look a bit young for Vietnam," Shaffer said.

"Desert Storm," Barto replied. "Piece of cake compared to your war, or so I was told."

"War is war," answered Shaffer. "No such thing as a piece of cake war."

Shaffer pointed at Laura and asked, "She yours?"

"No, she's just a good friend. Her mom is the singer you came to listen to. How about you, any kids?"

"I have a son, but if you ask him, he has no father. He thinks I'm a bum, and I guess he's right."

"At least he knows you. My son doesn't even know that I exist," Barto answered.

"We are quite a fatherly pair," said Shaffer, and Barto nodded his head in agreement.

Laura continued watching TV silently and the police show was now showing a military funeral with military honors.

"I don't suppose I'll even have anyone to come to my funeral," Shaffer said as he nodded at the TV screen. "It would be nice to have taps played though. Nothing need be said, just taps," he said as he drifted away. Most of the time, it was hard to tell when Shaffer lapsed into his inner world, but Barto could see in his eyes at that moment, his mind was a world away. Just as quickly, he snapped back and reached into his wallet. "Here, take this. Give this to someone if they want to read it when they bury me."

Barto took the old and creased piece of paper and nodded his head as he saw what was written. "I don't guess I know of anything to be said when I die," Barto said. "There's this old abandoned church I visit every once in a while, and I have family buried there. They can just scatter my ashes around there I suppose."

Both men turned their attention to the TV and compared notes about their military service. When it came time for the Waltmans to entertain, they sat together and brought Laura along. Barto could see that the Waltmans were popular here. They were very good, and they truly seemed to enjoy performing for the Vets.

When the entertainment was over, Barto helped clean up the kitchen, and he and Laura were ready to head back to the Waltman house. On the way back to his truck, Barto grabbed the last trash bag and dropped it into the dumpster out back. Shaffer followed them out and was greeted by a medium sized dark brown mutt of a dog. He limped up to Shaffer while wagging his tail excitedly.

"This is Kilroy. He's sort of the Center mascot." Shaffer unwrapped the napkin he was holding and offered Kilroy several pieces of leftovers he had confiscated from the kitchen. "He was hit by a car awhile back, but aside from the limp, he seems okay. He fits right in here with the rest of the walking wounded. He's harmless and very friendly," he said as Kilroy limped over towards Barto.

Barto started petting Kilroy, and Shaffer started walking out of the alley. "Can I give you a ride somewhere?" Barto asked.

"No thanks, I live just around the corner. Maybe I'll see you at the Center again."

Barto waived and replied, "Nice to meet you, I'll see you around I'm sure."

With Shaffer gone, Laura and Barto were alone with Kilroy who was now wagging his tail between them. Laura reached down to pet Kilroy and said "Poor Kilroy." When her hand touched his fur, she jerked her hand back and yelped.

Barto saw this and smiled, "You must have been shocked, it should be discharged by now "

Laura again reached down and stroked Kilroy's fur. Barto noticed her compassion as she cooed and encouraged Kilroy while lightly massaging his hurt leg. Eventually, she stopped her hands and gently held his hurt leg between both her palms. Kilroy remained still and content. Laura went silent and closed her eyes.

Several moments later Barto said, "We'll come back and visit him again, but we better get going."

Laura released Kilroy and stood up. "Goodbye Kilroy, maybe we can bring you some treats next time."

Barto took Laura's hand, and they walked towards the truck. When he noticed Laura walking with a slight limp, he asked her if she was okay. "I'll be fine I'm sure Mr. B," she said. He glanced back as he heard Kilroy running out the opposite end of the alley. Very strange he thought; Kilroy ran like an excited puppy, no limp and no hint of any hurt at all.

Chapter 10

THANKSGIVING

The Thanksgiving holiday at the Waltman Estate was a traditional family event including all four of the ladies along with Valentine and his family. On Thanksgiving Eve, everyone gathered in the kitchen area and made pies and other treats for the next day's feast. Eventually, the adults sat in the "Room of Souls" with their coffee and pie while Rasheem and Val's sons camped out for their overnight sleepover in the greatroom.

Elizabeth reminisced, "Mr. B, before you joined our family, I guess Rasheem was our latest Thanksgiving dinner addition. His mother and I had just moved in together when she was killed in a car accident. Being around Val's kids sure has helped him along the way."

From previous conversations, Barto knew that Elizabeth was a lesbian and that her friend Rosanna and her were a couple. She had explained everything to Barto one night when they were talking about Rasheem and how he had come to live in their home. She made light of the tendency of everyone around her whispering the word "lesbian" as if no one else should hear.

Thanksgiving Day began as Susannah fussed around in the kitchen, checking on the food and the table preparations. Margaret, Elizabeth, and Sarah had gone over to the Veteran's Center to help prepare an early Thanksgiving meal. Val and his wife had come over early to help Susannah and rescue the family from their two boys.

Barto had offered to help Susannah, but was strongly rebuffed with a friendly but stern smile. He had promised Laura that before dinner, they could get together in the workshop to finish a special project she had been working on.

Barto gathered Laura and went to the workshop to finish the holiday windchime gift to her family. He had already cut the sail for the chime that Laura wanted to give to the Waltman ladies. Over the last few days, she had painted the turkey-shaped sail, the striker ball, and the wooden cap. Barto had cut the metal pipes and drilled the holes in all of the necessary parts. Today, Laura would string those parts together while Barto used a wood burning tool to write Laura's message on each side of the sail. He burned 'Mommy & Grandma' on one side and 'Aunt Maggie & Aunt Lizzie' on the other side.

"Thank you for helping me with this Mr. B, I hope they like it."

"I know they will love it Little One, especially since it's from you."

"I'm thankful for you too Mr. B, you're my Nudge after all."

Barto was still not totally comfortable being

considered Laura's Nudge, so he replied with a simple "Thank you."

"When you were a little boy, did you have Thanksgiving with your family?" Laura asked.

"This was always my favorite holiday," he replied. "Whenever we could, my mom and dad and I would visit my mom's parents, and we would have a big dinner, eat lots of pie, and sit around and watch TV. My father's parents lived about an hour away, and we would visit them a few days later. We had two big Thanksgiving dinners in just a couple of days. My father and uncles would throw the football around with me and my cousins. I know they liked throwing us the balls as much as we liked catching them. It's been a long time, but I still remember the fuss my father would make when we made a good catch. He always made me feel important." Barto fell silent while reflecting on his early holidays. He stared blankly at the turkey windchime.

Laura's voice brought him out of his stupor. "I bet he was a very nice man. I think we would have been good friends, just like you and me." Barto simply nodded and resumed his work on the chime.

By the time Sarah came out to the workshop to fetch them for dinner, the windchime was finished. Laura had wrapped it in an old newspaper and put it into a previously discarded plastic bag. She carried it in one hand while her mother led her to the house with her other hand. When her aunts insisted on opening the bag before they got to the dining room, both Margaret and Elizabeth made a happy fuss over their names on the chime. Susannah added the chime to her porch collection and gave Laura a smothering hug.

Before everyone settled in for dinner, Val was asked to say a prayer of thanks. He spoke clearly and confidently while giving thanks for their bounty of food and thanks for the company of family and friends. He ended by thanking God for bringing their new friend, Mr. Barto, into their lives and to bless him and protect him too. After the family repeated the Judge's "Amen," they dispersed to their assigned places.

Rasheem and Val's two boys were allowed to get their food and eat on a special table placed in front of the TV. Barto stayed quiet, but noticed that he was assigned to his normal place of honor at the end of the dinner table. Val sat at the other end of the table, and he began the distribution of the turkey he had carved minutes earlier. Val's wife took Rasheem's normal table spot, and everyone else headed to their normal seats. Laura, however, moved unusually quick and smoothly and without permission, sat in the chair next to Barto. Sarah was amused and dutifully accepted the seat between Laura and Susannah. "I guess I can share you with Mr. B Laura," she said as she settled in.

The dinner conversation was light and informal as everyone filled up on the special meal. Barto was polite, but quiet, and seemed a bit distant. When the meal was over, all the ladies cleaned off the table and started washing the dishes while enjoying each other's company. Laura joined the boys in front of the TV, and Val chaperoned the kids while taking a nap on another sofa. Barto headed down to his room with the intention of following the Judge's lead of taking a post-meal nap.

Several hours later, the Waltmans set up for an evening meal of turkey sandwiches and other leftovers from the earlier formal meal. Sarah went down and gently knocked on Barto's door to let him know that the food was ready if he was interested. He didn't respond so Sarah left him alone to finish his nap, knowing he could eat anytime he wanted to.

The next morning, when Barto didn't appear for his usual morning coffee, the Waltmans assumed that he wasn't feeling well, or maybe he was just sleeping in over the holiday weekend. They knew he would reappear when he wanted to, and they wanted to continue to respect his privacy. However, when Val dropped by in the late afternoon, Susannah couldn't help but mention Barto's absence.

"I'll peek my head in and see if everything is alright," he said. When he came back up the stairs, he reported, "He's not in his room, and I'm not sure he was there last night either. His towels aren't used, and his bed looks unslept in. Did you check to see if he was in the workshop?"

Barto had moved his truck to the far side of the garage to stay out of the way of the increased holiday parking lot traffic. Elizabeth sent Rasheem to check on the workshop and Barto's truck. He reported back that the truck was indeed gone. Susannah began to worry and asked her daughters where they thought he might be for that period of time.

Margaret suggested, "Maybe we should try the Vet Center. He and Corporal Shaffer have gotten close lately."

Val made the call to the Center and even talked to Shaffer. "He was here yesterday evening to say hi and pick up a couple of things, but I haven't seen him since," said Shaffer.

"I'm a little worried Val," said Susannah to her son. "Should we call the hospital?"

Val thought for a bit and replied, "Let me try one other thing first," as he picked up the phone. "Sheriff Bastian please, this is Judge Waltman." The Judge waited while the connection was made, and after being routed to Bastian's cell phone, the Sheriff answered. The Judge could tell that he was driving. "Bobby, this is Val, I hear you're out on the road. I need a favor…"

Chapter 11

FADING AWAY

Sheriff Robert Bastian knew the White Deer Valley quite well. As the County Sheriff, he visited the jails often. They were installed before he was born, but even before they were built, his ancestors had lived here, and many of them were buried here. He had made it a point, even as a young man, to research and track the local genealogy of his family, and much of that originated in this valley.

Today he was headed out to the Old Stone Church as a favor to his friend Valentine Waltman. Val was now a County Judge, but they had met and become friends when the Judge was a young lawyer and the Sheriff a young deputy. Val had called him and asked him to check out the church area to see if Samuel Barto was there. The Judge confirmed that this was the same Samuel Barto that Bastian had found by chance a few months back in the church cemetery with a self-inflicted gunshot wound.

This area was practically deserted, and only the prison maintenance crews came here to mow and landscape the cemetery and church grounds. Bastian had always enjoyed the peace and quiet here and tried to drive through whenever he could, but he knew that Barto was lucky that he happened to be driving by that day or he would have bled to death. Or was Barto unlucky, thought Bastian, considering he was trying to kill himself anyway?

It was already dark as he came to the top of the hill that the church and cemetery stood on. To the left of the small dirt road stood the Old Stone Church which was in remarkable condition considering it had no regular congregation for over 70 years. The 110-year-old building was well cared for by the prison staff, especially during the last 30 or so years after community activists had raised a stink about its neglect.

Barto's truck was parked in the gravel parking area to the side of the church in the illumination of several streetlights. Bastian parked next to the truck and confirmed that this was the same vehicle he had found here when he had originally found Barto. When he checked inside the truck, he noticed that the bed and the cab of the truck were empty. On a quick glance around the area, he noticed what seemed like a campfire over in the cemetery. As he walked closer, he saw the figure of a man sitting next to the fire, poking at the flames. He was obviously alive and breathing. Bastian retreated to his car and called Val to let him know that Barto was indeed here and seemed to be okay. The Judge asked him to keep an eye on Barto until he could get there, and the Sheriff agreed.

Barto heard and then saw the Sheriff's vehicle when it came up the hill. The Sheriff represented the only human that Barto had seen since he came here yesterday.

The bright moon made walking through the iron cemetery gate quite easy, and the prison maintenance crews had made it easy to navigate through the headstones and exposed tree roots.

Although this cemetery pre-dated the existing church by nearly 100 years, it was still small and easy to get around. The last burial here was over 50 years ago when a wife was finally allowed to join her late husband. Barto heard the visitor walking up, but continued to gaze at the fire while adding some loose twigs now and again.

"Good evening sir," Bastian said to break the silence.

"Good evening," replied Barto as he lifted his head to acknowledge the man. He noticed now that the man was a police officer, which made sense to him considering the time and location. "Are you here to arrest me sir?"

Bastian chuckled and replied, "I don't think so, but to be honest, I've never come across this situation before. Is it okay if I sit down for a bit?"

"Certainly, my name is Samuel Barto," as he offered his hand.

"Robert Bastian," he said as he shook Barto's hand. "We actually met out here once before, a few months back. I'm the one that found you," he spun to his right and pointed to a nearby bench by the fence line, "Right over there I think." Barto nodded his head, but did not respond to the awkward moment.

Bastian did not mention that Judge Waltman was the one who sent him here and that he was on his way. He knew that Barto had been staying with the Waltmans and was helping them out as a caretaker. By all accounts, he was doing well, so he didn't want to make any assumptions on Val's current interest or the circumstances that brought Barto here.

Barto didn't know if he should thank the Sheriff for finding him here those many months ago and basically saving his life, even though he was trying to kill himself, so he decided to just keep quiet.

"Do you have your gun with you this time Mr. Barto?" asked the Sheriff. The question was meant to confirm his own safety as well as Barto's.

"No sir, I left it back in storage. I have no plans to shoot it out here."

It was then that Bastian noticed the empty liquor bottles on the ground next to Barto's leg and the other half empty bottle propped up between his knees.

Barto caught his gaze and looked down at the open bottle. He knew he shouldn't offer any to the uniformed officer. "I don't even drink, at least not till today I guess." He perked up and said, "In fact I think I might be drunk. Believe it or not, I've never even been close to drunk until now, it kind of feels… different."

Bastian smiled as he watched Barto inspect each finger as he slowly wiggled them closely in front of his eyes and then dropped his hands to his sides.

"That's a nice fire on a cool evening," Bastian said. "You didn't cut down any trees or anything did you?"

"No sir. I just picked up some loose stuff that's all around the outside of the fence." Barto pointed up and down the large path where he was seated. "I built it here on this path. I figured they used it when they came with the horse and buggies and the caskets and the visitors a long time ago." He pointed to his right and added, "Near my family."

"I have family up in here too, in the middle," Bastian said as he pointed towards the middle of the small cemetery, near the grove of trees. "I've been coming up here since I was young. It's very peaceful up here. I like looking for the turkeys and deer and the other wildlife. I swear I even saw a bobcat once, but no one believes me."

Valentine Waltman had never been to this part of the prison property, but as he drove up the small hill towards the church steeple, he knew that this was Barto's church. Barto had painted a very distinct picture of the area when he had described it to the Judge. When he made it to the top of the hill, he saw Barto's truck and the Sheriff's cruiser sitting side by side. Once he had parked next to them, he looked around and quickly noticed Bobby Bastian waving his hand across the road from inside the cemetery fence.

As the Judge walked up to the fire, Barto slurred slightly, "The Sheriff said he wasn't going to arrest me Judge."

Noting Barto's condition, the Judge said to Bastian with a slight smile, "Well thank you Sheriff Bastian, I appreciate your kindness to my friend." To Barto he said, "It looks like you've been drinking a bit Sergeant Barto. Are you trying to keep warm?"

"No sir," Barto replied, "the fire is doing a fine job with that, and I'm almost out of what Shaffer gave me anyway. I've never been drunk you know, but it seemed like a good idea at the time."

"Well then, maybe it's time we got home," the Judge said. "You can ride with me, and I'm sure the Sheriff will see to it that your truck gets home okay, won't you Sheriff Bastian?"

Bastian nodded his head, but before he could verbally agree, Barto spoke up, "I don't think so Judge. I don't think I can go back."

Bastian and the Judge sat down on the log surrounding the fire and thought about the situation. The Judge said, "What were your intentions when you came out here Sergeant Barto?"

Barto sat thoughtfully for a moment before downing the final drink from his last liquor bottle. "Thanksgiving was always my favorite, but yesterday reminded me that I have no real home. When my father was a Marine, we moved around and never stayed in one place too long. When I was in the Army, I moved around and never stayed anywhere for very long either. Your family has been the best thing that ever happened to me, but I guess I'm just not very strong. I don't think I can handle it anymore. I'm just a broken down old man and this place is the only place I've ever felt like I belonged. Maybe I just thought I could sit here until I faded away, like a good soldier."

When they heard the Waltman's passenger van coming up the hill, the Sheriff and the Judge stood up and started walking towards the church. Barto stayed behind and threw some more sticks on the fire.

Margaret was driving the van with Susannah riding shotgun. Laura sat between Sarah and Elizabeth in the backseat. They had dropped off Rasheem at Val's house to stay with the boys. At the top of the hill, Susannah noticed and pointed out the vehicles over by the church. Margaret pulled next to Barto's truck just as Val arrived with the Sheriff close behind.

Barto watched numbly as he saw the Waltman ladies get out of the van. Susannah gave Bobby a hug, and he shook the sisters' hands and patted Laura on the top of her head. He couldn't hear their conversation, but he could imagine what they must be saying about him. He had grown to love the Waltmans during the short time he had known them, but now he wished they would just get in their vehicles and leave him here.

One figure broke from the Waltman pack, but from this distance, Barto couldn't make out who was walking over towards him. The rest of the group kept up their conversation.

"Well we're not leaving him here," Susannah said to Val.

"Of course we're not Mom, but I'm telling you what he said, and I'm not sure how we're going to get him to come back home with us. He's technically not doing anything wrong."

Sarah was quietly listening to her family discussing their options. When she instinctively reached for Laura, she noticed she was away from her side. "Laura?" she said as she looked for her between the four parked vehicles. It was then that she and the rest of the group noticed Laura walking toward the campfire on a path lit by the streetlights and the unusually bright moon. She was about 50 feet away from them when Sarah started towards her to bring her back.

"Sarah," said Susannah as she reached out her hand. "Let her go," she said as she grabbed and held her youngest daughter's hand.

The entire group fell silent as they watched Laura walking towards Barto and the campfire. She was looking straight ahead at Barto's position, but made a deliberate turn through the cemetery gate and maneuvered around the headstones towards the fire.

Barto noticed that it was Laura when she reached the road. He stood up in silence as she made her way through his family monuments until she held her hand out to the broken old man.

"You have a very lovely church Mr. B," she said as she took his hand and sat next to Barto on his log.

The Waltman group could not hear any conversation from this distance, but they marveled at the precision of Laura's walk through the headstone obstacle course. They could see Barto well enough to see him stand and take Laura's hand. After several peaceful moments sitting on the log together, the pair got up and walked a few steps until they stood in front of a particular group of organized headstones.

Bobby squinted and said "I think that's his family's headstones they're standing in front of. Do you suppose he's introducing her to his ancestors?"

The rest of the group were also staring at the two figures, but remained silent.

"I wonder what it was like back then," Laura said. "I bet your great-great-great grandfather was the nicest man. He probably carried around candy in his pockets so he could give it to his grandchildren, and he probably had lots of horses that he let them ride all the time."

Barto enjoyed listening to Laura's voice, and he let her ramble on.

"I'd like to see my grandfather's headstone one day. I bet he was a good man too."

Shortly after he and Laura had returned to sit on the log in front of the fire, Barto noticed another figure from the parking lot group making its way towards the fire, and Laura soon went quiet.

Susannah Waltman slowly made her way across the road and through the headstones and didn't say a word until she sat down on the log next to Barto on the other side from Laura. She put her hand on his hand that was resting on his leg and said, "Your church is beautiful Mr. Barto. I look forward to seeing it in the daytime light."

Barto couldn't bear to look at Mrs. Waltman. He continued to stare at the fire and after several quiet moments, he said, "I'm very sorry ma'am. You've been so kind to me, and I've let you down."

"Nonsense Mr. Barto, you haven't let anyone down. You've been a blessing to us since the first day we met you," she said as she patted his hand. After a few moments she continued, "It's getting a bit chilly out here Mr. Barto, why don't you come home, and we can talk over some coffee and pie."

Barto still stared at the fire and replied, "I don't think so ma'am, I don't think I can."

After several more moments, Susannah stood up and said, "Very well Mr. Barto," and reached out her hand towards her granddaughter. "Come on Laura." Hand-in-hand, Susannah and Laura navigated through the cemetery and out the gate towards the group in the church parking lot.

Barto continued to stare at the fire, but he was now relieved that he could try and figure out his next move on his own. He could keep the fire going and get some sleep. He was suddenly very tired. Perhaps things would seem clearer to him after he got some rest.

Barto then heard a raised voice and looked up to see what was happening with the group still in the parking lot. He couldn't make out the voice or the words, but he knew that it was a voice of strength, not of yelling or anger. The group then seemed to disperse to the cars, and Barto heard the engines start up.

Val's car and the Waltman van backed up and went down the hill away from the church. When the dust had settled, Barto noticed the sheriff's car was running, but had not moved. Then he noticed the figure walking towards him with arms filled with what appeared to be blankets or coats. When he saw that Mrs. Waltman was carrying the blankets, he wondered why she was chosen to deliver the warm covers, but still, he appreciated the gesture on this chilly night.

When Barto stood up to accept the blankets, he said to Susannah, "Thank you ma'am, but you didn't really have to…"

Susannah handed him one blanket and kept the other one for herself. She sat on the log opposite Barto and said, "You're welcome Samuel." She then picked up a stray stick and started poking at the fire.

Barto realized she was not leaving and slowly sank back down onto his log. "Ma'am, you don't have to stay with me, it's getting colder for you, and I'll be fine here by the fire."

Susannah continued playing with the fire, and without looking up she said, "Of course you'll be fine, but I'm not leaving." She looked up and smiled into his eyes. "You're part of my family now Samuel, and if you're staying, then I'm staying too. That's what family does."

In a panic, Barto glanced over to the Sheriff's car and back at Mrs. Waltman.

Susannah noticed the glance and said, "Sheriff Bastian has agreed to stay a bit until Val and the girls take care of his family, Rasheem, and Laura. Then they'll be back here too."

Barto didn't know what to do and didn't know what to say. He sat staring at Mrs. Waltman's nonchalant handiwork in the fire. Finally, he said, "I would offer you something to drink but it's all gone; I'm sorry."

"Thank you Samuel, but I would have had to decline." She paused a bit before continuing, "When I told you that I wouldn't have been able to make it without my family after Poppy died..." Susannah straightened up on the log and said, "I'm an alcoholic Samuel, but I haven't had a drink in 20 years. I almost drank myself to death and still have times that I think I won't be able to survive without a drink. I leaned on my family then, and I lean on them now."

Barto looked at Mrs. Waltman with a look of shock and amazement. When she looked up and noticed the look, she smiled and said, "My girls told you a little about what they've been through, did you think I was perfect?"

"No ma'am..., I mean, yes ma'am I did," he stuttered. "When I look at you, I see the strongest, softest, and most caring person I've ever met."

She smiled, patted his leg, and said, "Thank you Samuel, but you better be careful what you say. I can feel a real big hug coming on."

For the next several minutes, Barto and Susannah sat quietly while enjoying the mesmerizing affects of the small fire. The combination of the hypnotic flames and his recent alcohol consumption opened up Barto's mind to memories he was rarely able to think about. Through his fire induced gaze, Barto finally said, "Mrs. Waltman, I don't know if I can ever talk about..." And he stopped.

"It's okay Samuel, you're family now, no matter what, and you don't have to say anything." Susannah then stood up and moved over to sit next to Barto on his log. She picked up his blanket and put it around his shoulders. "We've leaned on you a lot these last few months, Laura and Sarah especially. I suspect you're the kind of man that, all your life, other people have leaned on you too. Maybe it's time for you to have someone to lean on too."

"I'm not so sure about this whole Nudge business ma'am."

"Maybe it's your turn to get a nudge Samuel."

"I'm not even sure I believe in nudges ma'am. There's probably not a nudge big enough to help me anyway."

Susannah knew that reasoning with Barto at this time would probably not work, especially in his current condition. She was resigned to wait this out until a clearer head prevailed.

After the fire had burnt down to embers, Barto finally stirred and looked over at the Sheriff's still idling car. He said to Mrs. Waltman, "Do you think the Sheriff would mind driving us home now ma'am?"

Susannah grinned and stood up with Barto and said, "I think we could bribe Bobby with a hot cup of coffee and a piece of pie."

When they returned to the Waltman house, Rasheem and Laura were already in bed. At Susannah's request, Val and Bobby settled into the greatroom with Sarah and Elizabeth to enjoy their coffee and pie. Susannah and Margaret helped Barto down the basement steps and into his room. Barto was quiet until he said, "You know, I've never been drunk before Ms. Maggie, oops, sorry ma'am."

Margaret smiled and replied, "So I've heard Mr. B, and I hope this is your last time too. Now let's get you tucked in like my daddy used to do for me."

Susannah added, "How about you Mr. Barto? Did your father tuck you in at night too?"

By this time, Barto was in a sleepy stupor, but he had heard Mrs. Waltman's question. "My father was a great man ma'am. He played catch with me and played games with me, and he even served his country in three wars. He was my hero."

"He sounds like my Poppy. I think they would have been great friends," Susannah answered.

Barto was still and quiet and apparently had finally fallen to sleep. Margaret and Susannah finished up by draping his clothes over his chair and moved his shoes under his bed so he could find them easily in the morning.

"Good night Mr. Barto," said Margaret as she grabbed the door handle to leave.

"I killed him you know," Barto said suddenly.

Not fully comprehending his words, Margaret asked, "Excuse me Mr. Barto?"

"I killed my father," Barto slurred again. "Just as if I took a gun to his head and shot him dead."

The ladies heard the words and stood silently, Margaret's hand still on the bedroom doorknob.

"He was the best man I've ever known… and I killed him… and I couldn't even kill myself right. He would be so ashamed of me."

Barto's words faded at the end as he finally fell asleep, but the ladies had no trouble hearing what he had said. Margaret finally pushed open the door and together, mother and daughter walked out in silence.

Chapter 12

RIDING WITH DAD

There are no motorcycle helmet laws in Pennsylvania, but when Barto rode his bike, he always wore one or else he felt naked. As a young teenager, he rode a dirt bike, and wearing a helmet was mandatory for his safety. The thought of bugs and rocks hitting him in the face were other good reasons that he wore a full helmet.

Samuel's father always talked about his love of the motorcycles he rode as a young man. Ironically, Charles Barto didn't own one while his son lived at home. He explained later that with a wife and a kid and the rigors of work, he had other priorities and responsibilities that were more important than motorcycle ownership. He laughed when his friends suggested that he was full of bull, and the reason he didn't have one was because his wife wouldn't let him.

Until he was almost 13 years old, Samuel was indifferent about motorcycles, but that changed the day his father called him from work with a cryptic message.

"One of my work buddies just bought a big motorcycle, and he's letting me take it for a ride. I thought I'd come by and let you see it. Maybe you could get on with me, and you could get your first bike ride."

When Samuel digested his father's words, he became terrified. Knowing that his father was on his way home with a big, scary beast, he quickly ran and hid in his closet. Images of riding along and hanging on for dear life at 100 miles an hour drove him behind his hanging jackets and sweaters in the small, darkened room.

When his father got home, he settled the bike in the driveway and came inside with a big grin.

"Samuel! I'm here with the bike I want you to see!"

Samuel still cowered in the closet with the hopes that his dad would give up and go away. But Charles understood what was happening, and he changed his strategy.

He called out, "Come on out son, I really want you to see this motorcycle. I don't think you've ever seen one before. You don't have to ride it if you don't want to."

Samuel felt that this suggestion sounded like a reasonable compromise, and he didn't want to disappoint his father. He especially didn't want to seem scared in his father's eyes, even though he was.

When he made his way out of his hiding place, he met his dad at the parked two-wheeled beast, and it WAS big like his father had described. In fact, it was HUGE in Samuel's eyes. But his father hadn't mentioned all the chrome and the large double seat. It was love at first sight.

Charles looked over at his wide-eyed boy and

said, "Quite a machine, isn't it son?" He held out the second helmet he had brought along and said, "Wanna go for a ride? I'll take it nice and easy."

Samuel didn't answer his father out loud, but he found himself slowly reaching out for the half helmet his father had brought along just for him. He was still apprehensive about climbing aboard the mammoth machine, but he couldn't help but feel the excitement grow within him.

On the road, Samuel quickly lost his misgivings about the ride and was soon overcome with a rush that he has maintained on every motorcycle ride he has ever been on to this day. He wrapped his arms around the waist of his huge father and felt peace and security. When the ride ended and Charles dropped him off at their house, Samuel knew then that he was hooked for life.

For Samuel, his first opportunity to drive a motorized vehicle of his own came around his 13th birthday, during a special sale at one of the larger, local discount stores. His father saw a mini-bike in the store advertising flyer and went down early to wait in line for their opening. Samuel waited at home patiently. When he returned, Charles was empty handed, explaining that the store had sold out before he could get one. For one of the few times that he could ever remember, Samuel fled to his room and cried because he wouldn't get what he so desperately wanted.

A bit later while Samuel was still stewing in his room, Charles and his wife had a vigorous argument, and eventually the huge man got back in his car and drove away. Samuel hadn't even noticed he had left until he returned several hours later with a trailer hitched to his car. When Samuel looked outside, he immediately bolted out the door and ran to his father's side. On the trailer was a brand new dirt bike, just his size. It was way too small for his father.

"You're gonna have to be real careful when you ride this son, or your mom will kill me," Charles said as he loosened the straps holding the bike onto the trailer. He looked up at his son with a smile and repeated the thought, "Okay?"

During his last visit with his father, Charles had warned Samuel that he had a surprise to show him when he arrived from his then current duty assignment. When he lifted the garage door, Charles showed off his new, fully loaded Harley Davidson. Even though Charles seemed on the road to recovery at that time, he was physically half the man that he used to be. Samuel wondered out loud how his father could handle such a beast and questioned his reason for the purchase.

Charles replied, "Even if I don't ever ride it again, I've wanted one for a long time now. So I bought it now, in case I never get the chance again."

Samuel knew that answer wasn't a very practical one, but he understood, and with his father's blessings, took it out for a spin. When Charles Barto died, his motorcycle was still parked in his garage with barely a couple hundred miles on it. Samuel was still in the Army and still had his family to care for, so he reluctantly sold his father's motorcycle and continued to long for the day he would have his own.

After he had outgrown his dirt bike, Samuel wouldn't buy another motorcycle until he had retired from the military. It was a large street cruiser that he told himself was a retirement present to himself. Even then, he didn't ride as much as he would have liked, but when he did, he felt free and at peace. He knew that many riders enjoyed the companionship of others on their bike rides, but he rode mostly alone, enjoying the solitude of the moment.

While living with the Waltmans, he rode his bike more often than when he lived in the south, but more and more often he wanted to bring Laura along with him on his trips, so he took his truck. He was not comfortable enough to have her on the back of the motorcycle, and he wouldn't have the same opportunity to talk with her while she was encased in a helmet.

Soon, most of his motorcycle rides were limited to trips to his church. The ride to the valley was reasonably long and windy and gave him the opportunity to clear his head and enjoy the journey. No one else could see through his full faced helmet, but on every trip, he couldn't help but smile.

This was the feeling that his father had loved, and he had passed it down to his son. Samuel felt his father's presence every time he climbed aboard his bike and rode into the wind. He couldn't help but feel that his father was always along with him for the ride.

Chapter 13

CONFESSION

For several days after the Thanksgiving weekend, Barto busied himself by taking care of the Waltman van and their cars. Even though most of the yard work had passed with the season, he had plenty to do while cleaning and prepping the equipment for the winter. He was embarrassed by his actions over the weekend and did his best to stay away from the inside of the house and contact with the residents. When they did interact, both parties were cordial.

The Waltmans also did not go out of their way to interact with Barto, although their intention was to give him his space. They knew that a little time could get things back, or closer to normal.

Later in the week, Barto came through the kitchen sitting room on his way to the basement stairs. All the ladies were sitting down, each with a full coffee cup in their vicinity.

Barto said, "Good evening ladies, I hope it's okay

if I get a couple pieces of bread."

Susannah answered, "Of course Mr. Barto, you're always welcome to anything we have. In fact…," she said as she got up from her chair, "the coffee is fresh, and I just made some blueberry pie. Why don't you join us?" Susannah moved so quickly that she had a cup filled and into Barto's hand even before he could answer.

"Are you sure ma'am?" Barto asked. He felt uneasy and diminished in their eyes after his most recent behavior at his church and the comments he may have made when they had returned home.

Susannah smiled and pointed at his regular chair sitting empty in the corner. "Elizabeth, would you get the pie please?" she asked her closest daughter.

"Mmmmm, blueberry," Elizabeth said to the pie as she cut the first piece. Barto settled into his chair and took a sip of the coffee.

"My car runs great Mr. Barto, thank you," Sarah said politely.

"Yes, thank you Mr. Barto, all of our vehicles run great now," Margaret added.

Barto replied, "I just changed the oil and tweaked them a bit before winter gets here."

Everyone settled into near-normal comfort as Elizabeth passed out the pie to everyone present.

After finishing dessert, Sarah refilled every one's coffee cup and they all settled in to light conversation and polite quiet. After an especially long swig of coffee, Barto cleared his voice and sat up straight in his chair. Looking at Susannah he said, "I wanted to say I'm sorry for my behavior last weekend. All of what happened is not clear to me, but what I do remember was not appropriate and should not have happened."

Susannah also sat up in her chair and looked at

Barto. "We've already agreed there is nothing to be sorry about Mr. Barto. We're family here, and we're certainly not a perfect family."

"Thank you ma'am, but I may have said something..." He hesitated and stared at his feet. "Did I say anything about my father?"

"I seem to remember a little, but not much," Margaret responded in an attempt to deflect his embarrassment.

Barto knew that if he remembered right, only Mrs. Waltman and Margaret were present when he talked about his father, but he knew the family was close enough that they all knew what he had said. He took a deep breath and said, "I think I owe you an explanation."

"You don't owe us anything Mr. B," Sarah interrupted. "In fact, it's me that owes you an apology for forcing Laura on you and pressuring you for information."

"No ma'am," Barto quickly replied. "Laura and this family are the best things that have happened to me in a very long time." He straightened and looked directly at Sarah and said, "I love Laura, and I love talking to her. Sometimes I feel guilty that I can't share her voice with you, but I hope that will happen for you one day." Then he looked at Mrs. Waltman and said, "You've been open and honest with me and now it's my turn. After all, that's what family does."

Susannah smiled and nodded as she leaned back in her chair.

Barto hung his head in deep thought and then started talking in a slow, deliberate tone. "I can't even remember what I used to call my father. Pops, Dad, Father, or whatever, I just can't remember. I used to feel sorry for him. He only finished the eighth grade and he lied about his age to join the military when he was 16. He later got his high school certificate, but I always felt superior to him because I had my meaningless college degree." Barto looked up and smiled, "When I grew older, I came to realize that he was 10 times smarter than I'd ever be."

"He was a proud grandfather too. Adam was three when my father died. His eyes lit up every time he held him. And he was very proud of me when I joined the Army. Soon after I joined, he was diagnosed with stomach cancer, but during one of my trips back home, he told me that his treatments were working, and he seemed cancer free. Even so, he talked about what he wanted me to do if it came back."

"My mom died of cancer a few years before that, and my father took care of her till her end. He told me he didn't want to be like her when he died, and he made me promise that I wouldn't let it happen to him. I brushed him off and told him I would take care of the military honors when they were needed many years from then. But he still made me promise."

Barto settled back into his chair and didn't notice the nervous motion of his leg, even though he now stared directly at his feet. "A year or so later, I was stationed across the country when his brother called me and asked me where I was. I didn't know what he meant, but he said my father was in the hospital in bad shape. I didn't know. I got back as soon as I could and went right to the hospital. When I walked into his room, his eyes were open, but he was basically a vegetable. He didn't respond to me at all. He had given up… and I immediately remembered my promise to him."

The Waltmans all remained silent and stayed as still as they could out of respect for Mr. Barto. Susannah desperately needed to give him a hug, but she knew that would have to wait.

"I talked to the doctor the next day, and he told me the cancer was back and couldn't be fixed this time. And then he cried. He said he never cried like that for a patient, but my father was special to him. I couldn't cry, at least not then, but his doctor cried for him. He told me that my father may live a little longer if he wanted to, but he didn't think he wanted to…"

Barto went silent for a moment and then continued, still staring down at his feet. "And then he told me it was my decision whether to keep him on life support or not, and he cried some more. I was looking for a way out of my promise, so I asked him what he would do. He told me he would take him off life support and let nature take its course. I kept thinking about that damn promise I had made to my father. Deep down, I wanted to credit the doctor with the decision to remove life support, but I knew it was me who would sign the final authorization. I was never able to go back into my father's room. I just sat in the hospital lobby, and I waited for my father to die. They told me he never came out of his stupor, and he died the next day. I killed him, just like I promised him I would. His death certificate said the cause of death was stomach cancer, but I marked through that on my copy and wrote 'Suicide by Son'."

After a few moments, Barto shuffled his sitting position a bit and started up a bit livelier as he quickly looked around the room. "I busied myself with Army stuff, and then there was Desert Storm. I remember wishing that I could talk to him about being at war. With all that, and losing my family, I didn't focus so much on my father's death. Then about a year after the war, I read about a pill that could possibly reverse stomach cancer. I never found out how that worked out, but it suddenly threw everything back into my face."

"Every day since then, I think about what I did and try to think about what I could have done differently, but that always gets wiped away by my promise to him. There are days when I don't think I can live with the guilt anymore, but I can never finish. I managed to kill my hero, but I can't even kill his cowardly son." Barto shook his head and continued his downward stare.

In Margaret's experience as a counselor, she knew that many people, especially from the military, were too proud to initiate any request for help when they suffered from depression, and unfortunately, some of them didn't know the help even existed.

Sensing a slight break in Barto's mood, Margaret spoke up. "That's a lot to carry around by yourself Mr. Barto. Our family has always had each other to lean on. But there are a lot of programs available for veterans. Why didn't you ever tell anyone that you needed some help?"

Barto slowly raised his head and looked at Margaret and said, "I don't know ma'am, I guess because nobody ever asked."

Several moments later, Susannah broke the awkward silence, "Maybe we can lean on each other Samuel, you and an old woman alcoholic."

"And maybe a hypocritical suicidal counselor can lean in too," added Margaret.

"The sinful lesbian would like into that lean too," said Elizabeth.

"Let's not forget the unwed teenage mother with the autistic child," said Sarah.

The morning after his confession, Barto climbed the stairs unsure of what to expect. It had been several mornings since he had joined Mrs. Waltman for a morning cup of coffee. As usual, Susannah was busy in the kitchen and had Samuel's coffee cup out on the counter in position for a quick fill. After their normal morning pleasantries, things seemed to get back to the normal routine.

As he walked outside towards the workshop to start his daily chores, Barto thought back on the last few months after he had tried to kill himself. He felt very fortunate that he met the Waltmans and wasn't sure where he would be without them. He thought about what they had told him of nudges and the possibility of him being a Nudge to Laura. And he thought about his breakdown on Thanksgiving weekend.

As he opened the door to the workshop, he wondered if this was the beginning of the renewal of his life, or was it simply a shortcut to his long anticipated end? He didn't know whether to laugh or whether to cry. Mindlessly, he pushed at the hanging windchimes to make them sing.

PART
FOUR

Chapter 14

MILITARY HONORS

The months had passed quickly since Thanksgiving weekend. Barto kept busy clearing snow and ice from the sidewalks and driveways at the Waltman house and the Veteran's Center. He also focused on the interior of the house and its cosmetic needs. And even though he felt more comfortable with the Waltmans, he still had his good days and bad days. It did seem to help that he had become more involved at the Vet Center by assisting the Waltmans whenever they helped out there. On his more difficult days, he would visit his church and only missed a Sunday visit if the weather wouldn't allow it.

Barto's next project for the upcoming early spring days was to get out the landscaping machinery and prepare them for the upcoming season. On this day, however, he was reading a book and taking advantage of the quiet and ambience of the Waltman library in one of its big, fluffy, overstuffed chairs.

Susannah called from the kitchen, "Mr. Barto, could you give me a hand in here please?"

"Yes ma'am," he replied as he marked his book's spot and got up from the chair with a satisfied groan. When Barto walked into the kitchen, he found all the Waltman ladies, Rasheem, Laura, and even the Judge had snuck into the house without him noticing. They were gathered around what appeared to be a homemade birthday cake with one large lit candle.

"Could you help me cut this cake Mr. Barto?"

Barto knew it wasn't his birthday, but he didn't want to insult nor disappoint Mrs. Waltman, so he accepted the knife and didn't say a word.

Sarah said, "It's been one year since you've been with us Mr. B, and we just wanted to let you know how pleased we are that you are now part of our family."

"And there's never a bad reason for Mom's homemade cake," Val added with a smile.

After hugs from Susannah and all of the sisters, Barto started cutting the large cake. He was handing the first big piece to a fidgety Rasheem when there was a knock at the back door.

"Just in time for cake Bobby," Val said to the Sheriff as he opened the door.

"Thanks Judge, I was hoping to talk with Mr. Barto a bit." Barto and the ladies looked up from the cake cutting ceremony and held out a plate with a large piece of birthday cake.

"Mr. Barto, I'm sorry to tell you that your friend, John Shaffer, passed away this morning."

Barto slowly put the plate down, and he stared at the Sheriff. Susannah put her hand on his shoulder and joined Barto's stare in anticipation of more information from Bobby.

"He apparently died peacefully in his sleep of natural causes." Bastian paused as Barto lowered his gaze and remained silent. Without words, all the ladies put their hands on his arm in unspoken comfort. Barto looked up as the Sheriff continued. "I know you and Corporal Shaffer were close. I was hoping you would come with me to tell his son. Barto nodded his head in hypnotic agreement. After getting his jacket, Barto followed Bastian to his car.

On the way to Benjamin Shaffer's home, Barto explained to Bastian about the Shaffers' relationship.

"I can't imagine that," said Bastian, "especially since his father was a war hero." The Sheriff reached behind the front seat and pulled out two important looking cushioned certificate holders. Barto opened them up and examined them for the rest of the trip.

Bastian rang the doorbell at Benjamin Shaffer's house with Barto at his side. A tall, young teenager opened the door, and the Sheriff asked him if his father was at home.

Without acknowledging the Sheriff's question, he yelled back inside, "Dad, the police are here, and they want to talk to you. I didn't do anything wrong so they must be here to take you."

A tall, slender man came to the door and put his hand on his son's shoulder. From his facial features and body build, there was no doubt that this was John Shaffer's son.

"Can I help you?" asked Benjamin Shaffer.

The Sheriff began, "Sir, I'm Sheriff Robert Bastian, and this is Samuel Barto. Are you John Shaffer's son?"

"Good Lord, what trouble is he in now?"

Bastian replied, "Sir, your father passed away this

morning in his sleep. We haven't had a chance to go through all of his things, but we wanted to let you know so you could start planning his funeral."

Shaffer was briefly quiet as the Sheriff's words sunk in. "He was a veteran. They can do whatever they do to take care of people like him. He was nothing but a bum to me Sheriff. He couldn't keep a job, hell, he couldn't even keep his family together. The military will pay for his funeral right? I don't think I'll be able to make the funeral. We're very busy at work right now."

Barto interjected, "I'll take care of the funeral arrangements Mr. Shaffer."

"Sergeant Barto and your father were good friends," said Bastian.

"Your father was a good man Mr. Shaffer. I got to know him quite well," continued Barto.

Shaffer answered, "I'm sorry he's gone Mr. Barto, I really am, but I didn't know that good man. To me, he was nothing more than an occasional nuisance. I tried to get to know him, but he was practically homeless for as long as I can remember, and he would forget to show up for any family thing we tried to set up for him. He didn't even know what day was his grandchild's birthday."

Barto held out the 2 certificate holders and said, "I was going to present you these at the funeral, but since you might not be there… One is a Silver Star for acts of exceptional valor in battle, and the other is a Purple Heart. He was a hero Mr. Shaffer, and while he was helping his fellow soldiers, an explosion messed up his head quite a bit."

Sheriff Bastian spoke to the now silent Shaffer as he stared at the awards, "We'll let you know when the funeral is Mr. Shaffer. I hope you'll be able to get off from work."

Bastian and Barto drove back to the Waltman house in virtual silence. While sitting in the driveway, Bastian gave Barto the mortuary details so he could go over tomorrow and make the funeral arrangements.

"I didn't know the government paid and took care of arrangements for veterans," said Bastian.

"They don't really. They do pay for a small headstone, but I'll take care of the rest."

Corporal John Shaffer had no one else that needed to be notified of his death. His funeral and burial were held at Everest Cemetery in the veteran's section. Through a local Army Reserve unit, Barto arranged for taps to be played, and since he didn't expect a big turnout, Barto decided that he would be the one to read the old bent up card that his friend wanted recited as his eulogy.

Corporal Shaffer was buried on a warm and sunny, early Spring Day. More people had come to give their last respects than Barto had anticipated. Many veterans that were regulars at the Veteran's Center had been brought in by vans, mostly by the volunteers that helped out at the Center. Some other older veterans from the area also showed up after they had heard about Shaffer's recognitions through the local Army Reserve unit and other local military chapters. There were also a couple of childhood friends who had apparently joined the Army with Shaffer when they were young. They had lost touch when he seemingly disappeared after the war, but had seen his obituary in the local newspaper. Benjamin Shaffer, his wife, and his son occupied the front row of seats that Barto and the Waltmans had stationed next to the flag draped casket.

Per Corporal Shaffer's request, there was no

minister and no formal service. Sergeant Barto and the Army Reservist bugler folded the flag and presented it to Shaffer's son, who was also clutching the 2 certificates tightly to his chest. The bugler saluted Shaffer's son and said, "On behalf of the President of the United States, a grateful nation, and a proud Army, this flag is presented as a token of our appreciation for the honorable and faithful service rendered by your loved one to his country and his Army." Sergeant Barto then stepped forward and announced that per Corporal Shaffer's request, there would be no formal service, but he had asked him to read a note card, followed by taps.

Barto reached into his pocket and pulled out the worn out card that Shaffer had given him. He cleared his voice, glanced at the mostly standing crowd, and paused a bit to collect himself.

"I am an American Soldier. I am a member of the United States Army – a protector of the greatest nation on earth. Because I am proud of the uniform I wear, I will always act in ways creditable to the military service and the nation it is sworn to guard. I am proud of my own organization. I will do all I can to make it the finest unit in the Army. I will be loyal to those under whom I serve. I will do my full part to carry out orders and instructions given to me or my unit. As a soldier, I realize that I am a member of a time-honored profession—that I am doing my share to keep alive the principles of freedom for which my country stands. No matter what the situation I am in, I will never do anything, for pleasure, profit, or personal safety, which will disgrace my uniform, my unit, or my country. I will use every means I have, even beyond the line of duty, to restrain my Army comrades from actions disgraceful to themselves and to the uniform. I am proud of my country and its flag. I will try to make the people of this nation proud of the service I represent, for I am an American Soldier."

The Army Reservist ended the ceremony with a perfect rendition of taps. Throughout Barto's reading of the "Soldier's Creed" and the playing of the bugle call, the audience of family members and old grizzled veterans stood at attention, a bit taller and straighter than usual and nearly all with tears in their eyes.

After the funeral, the Veteran's Center volunteers held an informal reception for Corporal Shaffer at which his son, Benjamin, proudly displayed his father's awards. He pulled Sergeant Barto aside and thanked him for all he had done for his father. "Sergeant Barto, I didn't know; I've been such an asshole...," he said as he wiped back some tears.

Barto answered, "No one knew, Mr. Shaffer, until they found his awards in his belongings. He talked of you often sir, and how proud he was of you. But he knew he wasn't right, and he didn't want to burden you and your family."

When Barto and the Waltmans returned to their house, there were sandwiches and salads and drinks already prepared for a quick and easy meal. Susannah stepped forward and hugged the lady standing in the kitchen who was apparently responsible for the generous spread.

Mrs. Waltman turned and said, "Mr. Barto, this is my friend and AA partner, Patricia. She insisted on helping us out while we said goodbye to our old friend."

Barto said to Patricia, "Thank you ma'am," and for the first time since he could remember, he initiated a hug to both Susannah and his new friend.

Val and his family left soon after the meal, but

Patricia and the rest of the Waltman family sat around with coffee and dessert. Barto sat in his chair, sipping his coffee with a polite smile to the occasional passerby that interrupted his stare of deep thought. At the dinette table, Rasheem played a game of cards with Patricia and Elizabeth. Laura sat and smiled out the window as she watched the windchimes swaying in the light breeze.

Sarah and Margaret surrounded the sink while organizing some dishes. "Margaret, I'm worried about Mr. Barto. What do you think we should do?"

"It seems to me he's trying to hold together as best as he can," replied Margaret. "We just need to be here for him in case he needs us."

The front doorbell rang again as it had several times during the day from a select few well-wishers who knew about the passing of Barto's friend.

"I'll get that on my way out," said Patricia as she hugged her goodbyes.

Susannah took this opportunity to take a freshly brewed pot of coffee over to Barto and fill up his cup. "Can I get you some more pie Samuel?" she said as she sat in the chair next to him.

"No thank you ma'am," he said with a polite smile. "I've eaten so much pie I may not fit through my bedroom door."

She patted his knee in support and returned his smile and then looked up as Patricia walked back into the room with a huge smile on her face. She took several more steps in and looked directly at Barto, "You have a visitor Mr. Barto. I've put him up in the greatroom and told him I would come and get you."

Barto stared at Patricia's long grin, and his mind raced at who would want to come and visit him, perhaps a friend of Shaffer's, or another veteran who had seen his obituary.

As if she was reading Barto's thoughts, Susannah spoke up and asked Patricia, "Did he say who he was?"

Patricia took another step towards Barto and it seemed that her smile got even bigger. Finally she said, "It's your father Mr. Barto, I sat him on the big couch so you two could talk in private."

Barto's shock was short-lived, and he chuckled as he got up from his chair. "That's impossible ma'am, my father passed away over 20 years ago."

Undaunted, Patricia replied back to the smiling Barto, "Well sir, I don't know about that, but that's who he says he is, and I believe him. He is most certainly your father Mr. Barto; I could see you in his eyes."

Patricia joined the Waltmans in reserved silence as they watched Barto walk through the kitchen towards the dining room and the greatroom beyond. Barto was still slightly amused, but definitely curious at Patricia's observation. 'Who could possibly be this person who says he is my father?' he thought.

As he rounded the corner out of the kitchen, he quickly noticed a large man looking around the walls at Susannah's art work. When he sensed Barto's presence, he turned and faced him and stood up with a big smile. Barto had taken several steps through the dining room and then froze in his tracks.

"Dad?" he stuttered in a tone just above a whisper.

The big man's smile radiated. "Hello son," replied Charles Barto, Samuel Barto's father.

Chapter 15

THE VISITOR

It bothered Samuel Barto that he couldn't remember how he addressed his father when he was alive. To most of his friends and acquaintances, Charles Barto was "Chuck," a short but solid atypical marine who, thanks to his many years as a heavy truck mechanic, was as strong as he was humble. For those people who didn't know him, his physical strength and quiet personality were intimidating, but to his friends, he was a likeable friend with a huge infectious laugh. When Samuel saw him sitting on the Waltman sofa, he knew his answer right away. He had simply called him "Dad."

"Dad?" Samuel Barto said.

"Hello son," replied Charles Barto.

"But this is impossible. How can this be possible?"

Charles continued to smile and waved to his son, "Come here and sit down son." Samuel slowly walked to his father, and they both sat on the long sofa. "I've learned that nothing is impossible Samuel, but I'm only visiting; I cannot stay."

Samuel slowly reached up and touched his father's cheek, and then his arm, and then gently grabbed his leg. Charles laughed the huge laugh that Samuel loved to hear but hadn't heard in over 20 years. "I'm not a ghost son," he said.

"Then what are you …or who are you… how can this be?" Samuel asked in broken phrases.

"I'm not here to tell you all the secrets of life, and I can't wave a magic wand to make everything better."

"Then why are you here Dad?"

Charles lifted his head slightly and stared up as if looking for the answer in some distant memory. "Hmmm, let's see… 'I'm not even sure I believe in nudges ma'am. There's probably not a nudge big enough to help me anyway'," Charles quoted while putting his big hand on his son's shoulder.

Samuel paused briefly but then sat up straight and said, "Are you my Nudge Dad?"

Charles again laughed loudly and glanced over to the kitchen entranceway.

Rasheem was pushing restlessly through the Waltman group as everyone stood peeking around Susannah to get a better glimpse of Barto's father. Laura was in the back, standing silently. Suddenly, Rasheem broke away from the pack and walked deliberately towards the pair of Bartos on the couch.

Elizabeth yelled, "Rasheem!" in a loud whisper while reaching out for him, but didn't have the courage to follow him through the dining area and into the greatroom.

When Rasheem reached the couch where the Bartos sat, Samuel didn't know how to react.

Instinctively, he put his hand on the boy's shoulder and said, "Rasheem, I'd like you to meet my father, Charles Barto. Dad, this is Rasheem."

Charles reached out his hand to Rasheem and said, "It's nice to meet you Rasheem."

Rasheem ignored the outstretched hand and instead, reached over and poked Charles in his huge upper arm. "Are you an angel? Did Allah send you Mr. Barto?"

Charles chuckled and replied, "What do you think Rasheem?"

"I'm not sure sir, but…" Rasheem stopped and looked down at his hands.

Charles gently reached under the boy's chin and brought him eye-to-eye. "What is it Rasheem?" he asked.

When Rasheem looked into Charles' eyes, he seemed to gain more confidence. "My mother is in Jannah, that's a Muslim's heaven Mr. B," he directed at Samuel politely. "I was wondering sir, if you ever get to see her if you would tell her that I'm doing okay here. Miss Elizabeth is nice, and I like her a lot," he hesitated and then continued, "but could you tell her I miss her a lot, and could you make sure to tell her I love her a lot too? I didn't get to tell her that before she died."

Charles listened to Rasheem with an occasional nod and a subtle smile. "When I see her, I'll certainly tell her that Rasheem, but I want you to know something. She already knows that you love her, and she misses you a lot and loves you a lot too."

Satisfied, Rasheem turned and walked back to the kitchen entranceway with the biggest and brightest smile that Elizabeth had ever seen. When he arrived back at the Waltman group, she smiled down at him and put her arms around his shoulders as they turned back towards the Bartos.

"Dad, will you really see Rasheem's mom?" Samuel asked when he looked back at his father.

Charles smiled slightly and settled back into the sofa, but said nothing.

"There are so many things I should be asking you," Samuel said, "but I just can't think straight." Samuel paused and noted that this was the figure of his dad he fondly remembered. After he had started his treatments, Charles had lost a lot of weight and physically was barely half the man he used to be.

"I think of you a lot Dad. I should have been able to do something, or at least do something differently. I should have done so much more for you, and I should have done so much more with my life. I'm so sorry Dad. You must be so ashamed of me." Samuel slumped forward and put his head in his hands.

Charles sat up and put his hand on his son's shoulder. "I made you make that promise to me, and you kept your word even though I know it was a tough decision. And I'm certainly not ashamed of you. In fact, I'm really quite proud of the man you've become." He paused and then asked, "But that doesn't make it any easier for you, does it son? Maybe it's me that should apologize to you."

Samuel looked up from his hands and gazed into his father's eyes. "Since you've been gone, I just can't seem to stay focused on anything. I don't want to just exist. I want to have some reason to live. You always seemed to encourage me, but even now, I'm having trouble finding a reason to stay alive."

Charles looked deep into his son's eyes and said with a slight smile, "Everyone has a reason to live son. For some people, it's just harder to find. In fact, it can be a fine line between a reason to live and a reason to die."

This time when Charles looked up at the Waltman huddle, they jumped to life and shuffled into the kitchen like a group of excited kids caught in an act of mischief. The kitchen entranceway was now empty…, except for Laura who still remained there quietly. Apparently, she was left behind, and no one seemed to have noticed. And then she slowly started walking towards the Bartos in a gait similar to her travels at the church and cemetery on Thanksgiving weekend. Samuel saw his father's gaze and looked up to see Laura deliberately walking their way. Charles stood up as she crossed through the dining room and stopped in front of them at the greatroom's sofa.

Her face was filled with a bright smile as she reached out her hand to Barto's father. "It's so very nice to meet you Mr. Barto. Your son has told me so much about you."

Charles returned her smile with a similar broad grin and wrapped her extended hand in both of his big, strong hands. "The pleasure is all mine Laura."

Samuel noted that his father already knew Laura's name so there was no sense for further introductions.

"You must be very proud of your son sir; he is a very good man. He is very special to me."

Charles replied, "I am very proud of my son Laura, and I'm also very proud of you too."

Slightly embarrassed, Samuel added, "She is very special to me too Dad."

Laura looked down at her hands, which were still wrapped in Charles' huge hands. She looked back up and looked in his eyes and said, "Thank you for visiting us Mr. Barto. I had better get back to my mommy before they notice that I'm not there." She looked over at Barto and said, "Mr. B, will we talk soon?"

"Absolutely Little One, I can hardly wait."

Charles released Laura's hands and said, "Goodbye Laura."

"Goodbye Mr. Barto," she answered, and she walked back and disappeared into the kitchen.

The rest of Charles' visit was spent reminiscing about their father and son time spent together in the past. They talked about playing catch, motorcycles, the fun they had at Thanksgiving, and they even shared a few stories about each other's military service. These conversations were light and seemed designed to simply enjoy each other's company.

Eventually, Samuel grew extremely tired and closed his eyes for a short rest. When he woke up, his father was gone, and the Waltman family had all gone to bed for the night. He was covered with a blanket from his room, and his head rested on his favorite pillow. He decided to remain on the sofa and go back to sleep, and he didn't wake up until after the break of dawn.

Barto woke up the next morning to the smell of fresh coffee coming from the kitchen. He walked into the kitchen and was greeted by its sole occupant, Susannah Waltman. "Good morning Mr. Barto. I hope you slept well on that old sofa."

"Very well, thank you ma'am. That sofa is actually very comfortable." She poured him a cup of coffee, and they shared a quiet morning moment as they stood in the kitchen.

Barto didn't know what to think for sure about last night. Had he been dreaming? Were his meds causing real hallucinations this time? Or could his father's visit really have happened?

He tentatively said with a nervous smile, "I guess

I had quite a dream last night ma'am. I dreamed that my dad had come back to visit me, right there in your greatroom."

Susannah smiled and looked over her coffee cup, "Well Mr. Barto, if that was a dream, it must have been a very powerful one because I saw him too and so did my girls. And Rasheem is happier and more talkative than ever after talking to your dad."

Barto jerked his head up to look at Susannah to confirm her sincerity.

"But how?" Barto asked.

"Samuel, it doesn't take being a member of any certain religion to understand that if you believe that our Creator, who was powerful enough to create us and the entire universe, surely has the power to do anything. I may not be able to explain how, or understand why some things happen, I just know that with my God, anything is possible."

Now satisfied that his father's visit was not a dream, Barto followed Susannah out to the porch to enjoy his freshly refilled cup of coffee. As he blankly stared at his cup, he said, "There was so much I should have asked him, but for the most part, all we did was chit-chat... but it was a nice chit-chat," he said with an absent smile.

"Sometimes, talking it out is the best thing for a troubled soul, and to have someone else listen. Did he soothe any of your... concerns?" Susannah asked politely.

"I told him I was sorry, but he told me that I had done exactly what I had promised I would do. But I'm still guilty ma'am. I know it's what he wanted, and I know it was probably the right thing to do, but I'll always wonder if there was something else I could have done differently."

Barto finished his coffee and got up from his chair. "I guess it's time I got some work done. Thanks for the coffee and your shoulder to lean on."

"Anytime Samuel, maybe next time it will be my turn to lean on your shoulder."

As he was walking towards the workshop, Susannah said, "Samuel, can I ask you one more question?"

He stopped and silently turned around.

She continued, "Knowing what you know now, 20 years later. If you had to do it over again, would you make the same decision?"

Barto didn't have to think about his answer, he had been asking himself that same question for over 20 years now. "Yes ma'am, I would, I made a promise." Barto nodded confidently to Mrs. Waltman and then he turned back around and disappeared into Poppy's workshop.

Chapter 16

EVEREST

Everest is the largest cemetery in the county and by most graveyard standards, relatively new. It had started out as a small, non-denominational piece of land, safe from flooding and easily accessible. The veteran's section was added as World War II, Korean Conflict, and Vietnam War veterans began to pass away in greater numbers. Although not subsidized by the Federal Government, the local municipalities all pitched in to establish a very respectable final resting place for their honored warriors. The Veterans' Monument and Pavilion were later added through the fund raising efforts of many local veteran's organizations.

For several weeks after Corporal Shaffer's funeral at Everest, Barto's conversations with Laura included talk about his friend's funeral, as well as his father and grandfather and Laura's grandfather who were also buried in the veteran's section of Everest. Laura had often mentioned her desire to visit her grandfather's grave and eventually asked Barto if he would seek permission from her mommy. For his part, Barto had not visited his father's grave for awhile and saw no problem taking her along for a visit. He did not miss the irony of visiting the 20 year old grave of a man he had just recently spent the evening with in polite conversation.

When Barto asked Sarah for permission to take Laura to Everest, she agreed and in turn, asked if she could go along. "I'll give you plenty of space when we're there. It's just been a long time since I visited Poppy."

They agreed that the best time for a visit would be during the week so that there wouldn't be as many visitors, and Laura could possibly emerge from her own world to fully experience the visit. They decided to visit Barto's kin, Poppy Waltman, and Corporal Shaffer's newly planted headstone and then visit the Veteran's Memorial.

When they arrived at the cemetery, they parked the van in a strategically centered position from all their intended sites, but still far enough away that Sarah could retreat while Laura explored her surroundings.

Samuel Barto's grandfather, Charles Barto Sr. was one of the first veterans interred into the veteran's section at Everest. His simple headstone had his name, year of birth and death, and the unit he had served in during World War I. A brass flag holder specific to that war was posted next to the headstone with a bright new US flag proudly displayed.

Barto's father and Corporal Shaffer's graves were relatively close to each other, and they both had the same type of information etched into their headstones. Shaffer had a brass Vietnam War flag holder, and Charles had one for WWII, Korea, and Vietnam. Each metal memento held a crisp, new United States flag. It had occurred to Barto that his desire to be cremated and scattered across his church area site might eliminate the Persian Gulf War flag holder that he was entitled to when he died.

Poppy Waltman's grave was the closest to the Veteran's Memorial, and the farthest from the Waltman van. When they arrived at his gravesite, Sarah squatted down and brushed away the leaves and grass clippings from the headstone. Even though she knew that Laura probably couldn't hear her, she said, "Laura, this is your grandfather's headstone. I wish he could have known you. He would have loved you so much." To Barto she said, "Please tell her that Mr. B. I'm going to visit the Memorial and then I'll be in the van; take your time."

As Sarah walked towards the Memorial, Barto looked for signs from Laura that she was awake, but before too long he heard Sarah yell, "Mr. Barto!"

He grabbed Laura's hand, and they quickly made their way towards Sarah's voice at the other side of the Memorial wall. When they arrived, Sarah was kneeling down over an elderly lady who was lying against the backside of the granite wall. She was conscious but in pain and despair.

"Thank God you came by," the lady said. "I didn't know if anyone would ever find me." She pointed to her black and blue ankle and said, "I must have stepped in a hole while I was visiting my son's grave. He's the one over there." She pointed at a nearby stone with the name "Jerry Houser", with a Star of David on the stone. His American flag was held by a brass Vietnam Veteran's memento.

Sarah stood up and said, "I'll call an ambulance, my phone is in the van."

"No please," the lady said. "My name is Hannah

Houser and my son Reuben lives very close. He'll come help me."

Sarah accepted Reuben Houser's phone number and started a fast but cautious walk towards the van while trying to avoid the potholes and ruts in the cemetery's surface.

"I was cleaning off his stone, and I must have twisted my ankle."

Barto looked down at the injured ankle and wondered if she may have broken it by the nasty colors it was showing. He tried to think of something to relax Mrs. Houser and take her mind off the pain. He noticed some small stones on top of Jerry Houser's headstone. He asked, "Do you want me to clean off those rocks ma'am?"

"Oh no sir. It is a Jewish tradition for visitors to leave pebbles on gravestones to signify their visit. Jerry was killed in action in Vietnam, and many of his friends come by to pay their respects."

Sarah had reached the van and called Reuben Houser on her phone. He was already on his way, and Sarah agreed to stand by her van to show him the way when he arrived.

Laura had been standing quietly by Barto and Mrs. Houser until she slowly bent down to have a closer look at Mrs. Houser's hurt ankle. "I'm so sorry you hurt your ankle ma'am."

"It hurts a bit, but I'll be okay now that you found me, and my son will take care of me."

Barto glanced over as Laura reached down and touched Mrs. Houser's ankle. Both Hannah and Laura jumped back, and Hannah yelped slightly.

"I'm sorry ma'am," said Barto as he reached for Laura.

"No, it's okay. It didn't hurt. Her hands were a bit cold is all."

Laura looked up at Barto and collected herself and then sank back down over Mrs. Houser's ankle. Barto was ready to grab her, but something inside told him to wait. This time Laura very gently put both of her hands under Hannah's hurt ankle and held it in the palms of her hands. Hannah closed her eyes and inhaled deeply, but obviously was not in any additional pain.

"Oh my," she said as she opened her eyes and looked down at the little girl. Laura had her eyes closed, and Barto thought he could detect a small, brief grimace cross her face. After a few more moments, she opened her eyes and gently removed her hands from Mrs. Houser's ankle. She rose up and stood quietly after reaching for Mr. B's arm for support. Barto instinctively grabbed and held onto her hand and forearm to steady her stance.

Barto heard a car door slam, and he looked up to see Sarah and a man who must be Reuben Houser arriving at the Memorial. In anticipation of helping out his mom, Reuben had brought along a bag filled with ice.

"Mom, are you okay?" he asked. "Can you stand up?" he asked as he took her arm and helped her to her feet.

"My goodness," she replied as she stood and tested her ankle. She put her full weight onto her "hurt" leg and felt no pain.

Both Sarah and Barto leaned down slightly to examine Mrs. Houser's ankle and were amazed to see no bruise and no sign of any injury at all. They both looked at each other in shock, and Barto's gaze quickly darted towards Laura. She was standing quietly, seemingly in her own world, still with her hand on Barto's arm.

As Reuben took Hannah's arm and walked her to his car, she kept saying, "I thought I might have broken my ankle Reuben. It was all black and blue, and it hurt like the dickens. Ask them, and ask the little girl. She even held it in her hands and said how sorry she was that I was hurt. But then she let it go, and that's when you came, and now it feels fine."

Barto followed them to the van with Laura holding onto his arm and now walking with a noticeable limp. Sarah followed close behind and took notice of Laura's limp, but did not say a word. Reuben closed his mom's car door and also noticed that Laura was walking on a hurt ankle.

First the plant in the Heart Pot, then the dead butterfly on the workshop windowsill, and the dog at the Veteran's Center. And now Mrs. Houser's hurt ankle. Laura had touched them all, and they all had gotten better. Barto started to wonder how they were all connected.

Chapter 17

EMPATHY

The drive home from the cemetery was quiet. Neither Barto nor Sarah said a word, and Laura sat passively while looking out at the passing landscape. When they arrived at the Waltman house, Barto was the first to speak. "Miss Sarah, if it's okay, I'd like to take Laura into the workshop with me." Sarah knew that what he was really saying was that he wanted a chance to talk to Laura, and she readily agreed.

Barto and Sarah both noticed that Laura no longer limped as she walked into the workshop. Laura sat in her grandmother's rocking chair and played with a half-finished windchime that still had to have a sail assigned to it. Barto picked up several pieces of sketched out wood that he would eventually cut for sails, but he was distracted and had no intention of cutting them now. "Laura, do you remember visiting the cemetery this afternoon?"

"I do Mr. B. I remember the big wall and the nice

lady."

"She did seem very nice," he said cautiously. "Do you remember that she had hurt her ankle?"

"Yes I do, and it was all black and blue. I remember I felt sorry for her, so I reached down and touched her ankle." She giggled slightly and continued, "She said my hands were cold when I touched her, but it felt more like a tingle to me. It didn't hurt, but it did feel strange. You don't think I hurt her do you Mr. B?"

Barto smiled to reassure her and said, "No, you didn't hurt her, in fact, I think you may have helped her feel better. Do you remember holding her ankle with your hands?"

"I do remember. And when I held her ankle, I felt the tingle again, but this time it was much stronger. But then the tingling stopped, and I must have twisted my ankle too, because it started to hurt just like the nice lady. After that I stood back up, and the next thing I remember, I was here. My ankle is okay now though. It doesn't hurt at all."

Barto tried to make sense of what Laura had said and what she had done. Could it be possible that Laura's touch had healed Mrs. Houser's ankle? He remembered the words of Susannah when she said, "I know that with my Creator, anything is possible."

When Barto led Laura back into the house, Sarah took her hand and led her to the greatroom so she could watch the TV. She again noticed that her daughter was no longer limping. Sarah returned to the kitchen sitting room and her mother, her sisters, and Barto were already sitting in their now common spots. As she joined them she said, "I've already told them what happened at the cemetery Mr. Barto, but to be honest, I'm not really sure what I saw."

Barto tried to explain what he knew, "I should have told you earlier, but I was afraid you already thought that I was a nutcase. I didn't know what to make of it then, but I think she has done something like this before."

"Do you remember the Heart Pot you gave me when I first got here Miss Sarah? Laura touched the wilted plant on that first night we talked and the next day it was as good as new. Soon after that, she and I were in the workshop, and she held a butterfly that looked dead to me, and it got better right there in her hands and flew around the room. And do you remember the first day I visited the Vet Center with you? Kilroy, the Center's dog had been hit by a car and limped badly on his injured leg. As we were leaving, she touched and held his leg, and he ran away with no pain and no limp." Barto looked at all the faces around the room, hoping for their explanations, but they all simply stared back with anticipation of his next comments.

He continued, "I think when she touched them, they were all healed. And I think when she held Mrs. Houser's ankle, she healed it too."

Barto then related his conversation with Laura when they had come back from the cemetery, and then he stopped talking while he waited for their reactions.

Elizabeth looked over at a picture of a smiling Rosanna on the family memories' wall and said, "When his mother died, Rasheem was young, but he knew he had lost her, and he understood she wasn't coming back. After he came here to live with me, we all tried to help him feel welcome and loved in our family, but he had a tough time adjusting. There were days he would just sit and stare, and he would look so lonely no matter what I would do. I had almost given up that I could give him the kind of support he needed to move on."

Elizabeth looked over at Mr. B and said, "I remember a particularly tough day when it was just me, Rasheem, and Laura here while everyone else was out shopping for groceries. Rasheem was squatting on the floor staring at some toys in the library, and I had left Laura in the greatroom watching TV. As I was sitting there watching Rasheem and wondering what more I could do, Laura came into the room and sat down next to him on the floor."

Elizabeth paused and started to slightly shake her head. "I had never seen her do anything like that before without someone else's guidance. And then, still looking straight ahead and not saying a word, she put her head on his shoulder."

"Rasheem looked down at her and started crying as he leaned back into her. I got down on the floor with them, and we hugged each other until just before our family came home. It took awhile, but it seemed that from that point forward, he started to open up and get a little bit better each day."

Margaret stared forward as if she was visualizing her thoughts and said, "The night they found all my pills was the night I had given up on life, and I had decided there was no way I could go on. It was a night we were going to the Vet Center, but I feigned illness. When everyone left, I was lying on the couch, and Laura was up in her room. I had all my pills laid out on the table and even had it planned out in what order I would take each one. Just a moment before I had decided to take them, Laura came down the stairs and stood in front of me as I was sitting on the couch in front of my piles of deliverance."

Margaret paused to collect herself, and she looked

over at Sarah and then to her mom. "She just stood there staring at me with her little smile and her blank expression. We must have made quite a sight with her just standing there and me not knowing what to do. I couldn't say a word to her. When I looked at the pills again, she moved over and sat on the couch next to me... And then she leaned into me and wrapped her arms around me and she wouldn't let go. It felt like she was hanging on for dear life. Turns out, it was my dear life she was hanging on to."

Margaret added, "I thought it was a random act, and I didn't really understand what had happened." She looked over at Barto and said, "But maybe this was all a piece of a plan, and she nudged us just like you are nudging her now."

"Seems to me, there's a lot more to my granddaughter than meets the eye," commented Susannah with a smile.

Sarah spoke to Barto, "But why does she only talk to you and then only when no one else is around?"

Barto added with a small smile, "She talked to Mrs. Houser and my dad too, but I guess he doesn't count."

"You think there will be more?" asked Elizabeth.

Susannah answered, "Maybe, but maybe not, and we may never know the reason why either. Some things you just have to accept, even if you can't explain them."

Barto listened intently, but was still unsure of what his role would be in any upcoming events. He listened more as the ladies shared their thoughts and ideas with each other, but nothing definitive was ever agreed on. As the night grew late, he wished the ladies good night and headed down to his room. Halfway down the basement steps, he heard a hurried set of footsteps following behind him.

Sarah caught up to him as he was about to turn the doorknob to his room. "Mr. Barto, I'm worried about Laura and what she's getting into. What if she touches someone who's really sick, or badly hurt… or worse? I'm really glad you're with her Mr. B. Please take care of our little girl."

"I will Miss Sarah; you have my promise on that." Barto understood the significance of making a promise in this type of context, but he knew that he was a lot more comfortable when he made this one.

PART FIVE

Chapter 18

BEAUTIFUL SOUNDS

After the visit to the cemetery, Barto and Laura were even more inseparable. Every time they returned to the house from an excursion, the family would immediately search his face and ask him questions about Laura's latest feats, but nothing out of the ordinary had occurred lately.

Barto spent extra time at the Vet Center, fixing the old run-down building's problems as best as he could. For Memorial Day, he helped with the stage and podium at the Everest Veteran's Memorial as the area's distinguished visitors honored their local veterans.

In observance of the 4th of July celebration, the Vet Center itself would be hosting a show that included the Waltman sisters and recently retired veteran Harriet Harmon who had been a featured singer in the Air Force Band. She had spent 25 years with the band traveling around the world as an entertainer and ambassador for the United States military. When she retired to the area, she and the Waltmans became fast friends and co-entertainers at many Vet Center events.

As the Fourth approached, Barto and the Waltmans got busier with the preparations of the day's planned festivities. On the day before the celebration, Barto and Laura planned to drive to the Vet Center to make some last minute setups to the sound and light systems, and Margaret rode with them to be dropped off at Harriet Harmon's house for some last minute rehearsal practice. Margaret would be playing the piano as Harriet sang a new song that they were both very excited about.

"Please come in and be the first to hear our new song Sergeant Barto," Harriet said as she met them coming up the driveway.

Margaret added, "You'll be so busy tomorrow looking after things that you'll probably miss our show, but you have to hear Harriet sing this song."

Barto accepted politely, and with Laura in hand, they followed the musicians to the piano room in Harriet's house.

"Margaret, I have coffee made if you'll help me get it. I think I left the sheet music on the kitchen counter anyway."

Barto noticed the pictures of Harriet and her band mates standing among many dignitaries and significant sites around the world. He was fascinated by the pictures on her walls that included congressman and high ranking military officials.

"Take a look around Mr. Barto," Harriet said as she noticed his interest. "Those were some very good times."

When they had left the room for the coffee and sheet music, Barto's attention was centered on the room's walls. Laura sat at the piano and put her fingers on the keys without pressing down for the sound. "Do you think Aunt Maggie would teach me how to play one day Mr. B?"

"I think she would like that very much Little One," he replied.

Laura glanced over her shoulder as she sensed another person in the doorway on the opposite side of the room that Margaret and Harriet had exited. She politely stood up and made her way next to Mr. B. A girl about Laura's age entered the room.

"Hello, my name is Lydia Harmon, my grandmother is Harriet Harmon. I'm deaf so please speak to my face so I can understand you when you talk."

Barto noticed that despite another person's presence in the room, Laura was still awake and aware. He replied to Harriet's granddaughter, "Nice to meet you Lydia, I'm Samuel Barto and this is Laura. She's Margaret's niece."

Lydia took a seat at the piano and started playing with the keys, although it was obvious she had not mastered the instrument. "Gramma says that Beethoven was deaf and he was a great musician." She turned back around and faced Laura. "Do you play an instrument Laura?"

"No," she replied, "but I hope my aunts can teach me one day."

Lydia waved her over to the piano and said to Laura, "Come over here, and I'll teach you how to play chopsticks."

Excitedly, Laura went over to the piano, and Lydia reached for her hand as she said, "Let me show you where to put your fingers."

As their hands touched, they both recoiled in surprise. Lydia giggled and said to Barto, "It's funny

151

sometimes when you touch someone, and you get shocked."

Laura and Barto stared at each other until Laura looked away and then directly at Lydia. "Have you always been deaf Lydia?" she asked.

Lydia smiled back and said, "Most people are afraid to ask me anything about me being deaf, but I really don't mind talking about it. When I was 6 years old, I had an infection. It got really bad, and it took away my hearing. Gramma says that's why I don't sound like most deaf people, because I once could hear myself talk."

Again, Laura glanced at Barto with a slight smile and then faced back to Lydia. "May I touch your ears?" Laura asked.

"Of course," she replied, "but they feel like everyone else's ears, I just can't hear with them."

Barto stared at them with an equal mix of apprehension and fascination as Laura reached up with both her hands and gently touched Lydia's cheeks, and then caressed her ears. He watched as both girls closed their eyes for several moments until Laura finally let go and stepped over to Mr. B's side in silence.

Harriet walked into the room with Margaret close behind. "Sorry we took so long Mr. Barto. Here's your coffee. I see you've met my granddaughter."

Barto smiled as he accepted the coffee cup, but his attention remained on Laura as she stood quietly by his side with her eyes still closed.

Margaret sat at the piano and adjusted the newly reacquired sheet music. "I hope you like this Mr. Barto," said Harriet.

As Margaret started playing, Barto noticed Laura's eyes were open, and Lydia's eyes popped open at virtually the same time. She slowly reached up and cupped her ears as she turned to face her grandmother.

Harriet started singing and was through two impressive verses when Lydia ran over to her grandmother and grabbed her arm. "I can hear you Gramma, I can hear the piano and I can hear your beautiful voice!" she exclaimed.

Harriet stood in shock as she cupped Lydia's ears in amazement. Margaret stopped playing and stared. "How can that be? That's wonderful! Can you hear me say your name? Lydia, Lydia, Lydia, can you hear me?"

"Yes Gramma, I can still hear you!" she replied with a big smile.

"But how? It must be a miracle!"

"I don't know Gramma. Laura and I were talking, and she wanted to touch my ears. The next thing I know, I could hear Miss Margaret playing the piano, and then I heard your wonderful voice."

Barto and Margaret looked at each other and then looked over at Laura, who still stood quietly next to Mr. B.

Lydia reached up and touched her grandmother's lips and took her face in her hands. "Please sing some more Gramma. Your voice is so beautiful."

Margaret was now staring at Lydia but was too stunned to accompany Harriet, so Lydia's grandmother looked Lydia straight in her eyes and started singing the song a cappella. Although her full attention was focused on her song to Lydia, Harriet glanced over at Barto and Laura as he led her out of the house towards his truck. Halfway down the driveway, Laura looked up at Barto and smiled.

Barto said, "Laura, did you hear what just happened to Lydia? You made her hear again," he said excitedly. "You can hear her grandmother singing to her now!"

Laura shook her head and replied loudly, "I'm sorry Mr. B, I can't hear you," as she pointed to her ears.

Barto could now hear Margaret's piano playing begin as Harriet's voice flowed out of the house. He took Laura's hand, and they returned to the truck.

When they arrived at the Vet Center, Barto rushed through his work while at the same time, keeping an eye on Laura who was parked in front of the TV. There were volunteers in the kitchen, but he and Laura seemed isolated from anyone else, and she remained cognizant yet silent. As soon as he was done, he and Laura started back home.

When they arrived at the Waltman house, Barto looked over at Laura, who was looking out the window of the truck, and asked, "Can you hear me now Laura?"

He was relieved when she turned to him and replied with a smile, "I can hear you now Mr. B."

"I was getting a little worried Little One, but I'm glad you can hear again. Do you remember what happened at Miss Harriet's house?"

"I remember talking to Lydia, and then I touched her ears, and then we were outside, and I couldn't hear you. Is Lydia okay Mr. B?"

"When you touched her ears, you made her hear again."

"Then we did another good thing didn't we Mr. B? I'm so glad you're here to be my Nudge."

Barto hadn't thought about the healings as a team effort, but it was obvious that Laura thought so. He had to admit to himself that she probably wouldn't be able to do these things without him here. Still, this business of him being some kind of Nudge was somewhat disconcerting.

When Barto and Laura walked into the house, the Waltmans all had huge smiles on their faces, but Sarah's seemed a bit more reserved. When she took Laura's hand from Barto, she looked for an answer from his eyes.

"She's fine Miss Sarah," he said. "Laura is just fine."

As Sarah led Laura up the stairs to their room, Margaret burst out, "That was amazing Mr. B."

Elizabeth added, "Margaret told us everything that happened!"

Margaret continued, "To see that little girl hear again…she was so happy, and her grandmother… Mr. B, you and Laura are a miracle."

"It's Laura that is the miracle. I just stand there and watch her," Barto said.

Susannah walked over to him and gently grabbed his arm. "But without you Samuel, she wouldn't be able to do any of these amazing things. And even if you and Laura never help anyone else, you've already had a big impact on many people's lives."

Barto listened, but had nothing more to say. This time it was he that put his arms around Mrs. Waltman in a soft but firm embrace. He knew that he needed to feed off of her strength for whatever may come next. For Laura and him, the future seemed to be filled with promise and uncertainty.

Chapter 19

LESSON NUMBER ONE

Even as a young child, Sarah Waltman was an avid reader. Some of her favorite early memories were when she was seated on her father's lap as he read to her. She remembered being too young to understand the words on the page, but the pictures on each page and her father's soothing voice made the story come to life.

Sarah learned how to read quickly, and when Poppy was gone, she would sneak into the library and search for the books he had read to her. She would sit for hours reading the same books that he had read to her while imagining his comforting voice clearly pronouncing every syllable.

As a mother, Sarah took every opportunity she could to sit her daughter on her lap while she read, and pointed, and explained the words and pictures to her little girl. She realized that Laura probably did not hear or understand her while she was in her dream world, but she did seem more animated and excited when she had a book in her hands, especially when she was sitting in her mommy's lap.

Barto noticed that Laura started bringing books with her when she was spending time with him. Sarah knew she could enjoy them while she was in the workshop with Barto while he puttered around with his windchimes, or when he worked on other projects. She picked out the ones with a lot of colorful pictures, and Laura was content to share light conversation with Mr. B while she looked through her books in her grandmother's rocking chair.

Sarah would give Laura the books she knew were her favorites. When Barto saw that the books she brought to the workshop were mostly pictures with just a few easy words, he suggested to her, "Why not bring some word books next time, and you can read them aloud to me while I work."

"I wish I could Mr. B," Laura replied. "I really love books, but I can't read very well. I do like looking at these pictures, and I've figured out most of the stories with them and the words that I do know."

Barto was embarrassed when he remembered that even though Laura was almost a teenager who spoke very well and seemed normal in every way, her dream world had kept her from many opportunities, like learning how to read.

That same evening, when Barto and the Waltmans were gathered in the Room of Souls, he asked Sarah if she had more books with a few more words. "If it's okay with you Miss Sarah, I'd like to read some stories with her and eventually have her read some to me. I'm not a professional teacher, but we could start with easier words and work our way up until she can do it by herself. I think she would catch on very quickly."

Sarah immediately jumped out of her chair and hurried towards the library room. She called out excitedly, "I think that's a wonderful idea Mr. B! I'll get you the ones that I used to enjoy when I was first learning how to read."

Barto smiled when Sarah returned and handed him a huge stack of books that she could barely carry in one trip. He chuckled when he saw the bulk and said, "This should get us started very well."

"There's more when you get through these…" She stopped and turned towards her mother and her sisters who were looking at her and laughing out loud.

She knowingly smiled and blushed as she looked back at Barto while reaching towards the tall stack of bound stories. "I'm sorry Mr. B, but I think this is such a great idea. I guess I got a bit carried away."

Barto put his hand on top of the stack before she could take any books away and said, "This is fine Miss Sarah, I think Laura will be just as excited as you. She is certainly your daughter ma'am."

"That may be the nicest thing anyone has ever said to me Mr. Barto." She put her hand on his atop the stack of books. "Thank you for everything."

Barto hadn't said anything to Laura about his plan. He had wanted to make sure that her mommy approved. Sarah's excitement was contagious, and he really wanted to make this work. The next day, Barto made sure he got to the workshop well before Laura would arrive. He arranged a small rectangular table along the far wall near Mrs. Waltman's rocker, and he put two chairs underneath, side by side. On the back side of the table, against the wall, he divided the stack in more manageable piles and put one book out front in a spot between the two chairs.

When Laura came into the workshop later in the morning, Barto pretended to be busy on the bench. After exchanging pleasantries, he turned back to his work while peeking back to see her reaction.

"Look at all these books Mr. B. Were you planning to do some reading in your spare time?"

"Actually, Little One, I thought maybe WE could make some time to read together. How about if I teach you to read these books, and then you can read many, many more. I'd like to hear you read them to me someday soon, if you would want to."

Laura jumped up in excitement and gave Barto a hug as he walked over to the table. "I would like that very much Mr. B! Thank you so much! When can we get started?"

"We can start right now if you're up to it. I've laid out our first one right there on the table. Your mommy suggested it and said it was her favorite book when she was growing up."

Laura sat down and picked up her first lesson. As Barto sat beside her at the table, she pointed at the front of the hardback children's novella. "The little girl seems very happy Mr. B. I think this will be a great start. What is the name of this book?"

Barto took the book and slowly opened it to the first page.

"The Book of Laura," he said with a smile. "Chapter One."

Chapter 20

CHRISTEAN

By winter, Susannah Waltman had almost completed her portrait of Samuel Barto. She had allowed no one the opportunity to see it and vowed that no one, not even Barto, would see it until it was done. Barto was camera shy, and Susannah had nothing but memory to go by, but she was pleased with how her project was progressing.

Over the years, she had visited the Capitol Art Museum to absorb its spirit and become motivated to complete her various projects. For the next two weeks, in addition to the normal exhibits, the museum was featuring the sculptures and paintings of Solomon Jarrett. The artist himself would be there on Saturday to speak and comment on his work. Susannah had become a fan of the artist through her visits and the features she had read in several art magazines. She asked Barto if he and Laura would like to come along as Laura's first immersion into the world of culture.

Laura was very excited about going, especially after seeing some of Solomon Jarrett's work in a magazine that Susannah had given to Barto. She especially liked the sculpture he had recently finished called "Christean". It represented Jarrett's 12 year old daughter and was obviously an inspired representation.

Barto read the article to Laura which included Jarrett's extensive work and also a short biography. He was a very generous philanthropist, most notably to children's groups. His wife had died at a very young age, and his only daughter was named Christean. It also mentioned that his work was without any religious overtones due to him being an atheist.

When they arrived at the Capitol Museum, it was packed with fans and others simply curious about the works of Solomon Jarrett. A large room was dedicated to his sculptures and another section to his paintings. It took quite some time for Susannah, Barto, and Laura to get inside, but they were eventually rewarded with an up-close look at Solomon Jarrett as he stood inside the roped off perimeter of his works.

Like many artists, Jarrett wore his hair long and sported a full complement of facial hair. He was well-dressed and handsome by most women's standards. He was also a very personable man who answered many questions from the museum guests, most of which were about his latest works. When Susannah's group eventually made their way to where he stood, she shook his hand and introduced a shy Barto and a silent Laura.

"Mr. Jarrett, this is my friend Samuel Barto and my granddaughter Laura. They, of course, like your sculpture and so do I, but as an amateur painter, I especially admire your paintings."

Jarrett politely shook Barto's hand and then

reached for Laura's hand too. The moment he touched Laura's hand, he knew she could not speak and felt slightly embarrassed that he didn't recognize that immediately. He was pleased, however, to have found a fellow portrait artist in Susannah and invited her to accompany him to the area where his paintings were displayed.

Barto said, "I think Laura and I would like to stay and admire the sculpture of your daughter Mr. Jarrett."

Soon after Susannah and Jarrett had disappeared into the painting gallery, Laura perked up and stared into the eyes of the sculpture of Jarrett's daughter. "She is beautiful, isn't she Mr. B?"

He nodded his head in admiration.

"Look at her eyes," she continued. "It's like she can see right into your soul. I wish we could get close enough to touch them."

A hand from behind them touched Laura's shoulder, and the attached voice said, "I'm afraid they won't let you touch the statue, but maybe you'd like to touch the real thing."

Barto and Laura turned to see the beautiful, smiling face of a young girl that was the exact image of Jarrett's sculpture. "I'm Christean, and yes, I'm the model for the sculpture. I'm told it's quite a likeness."

Barto looked closely at Christean's eyes and finally recognized that this beautiful little girl was blind. Her long blond hair was the exact length of the sculpture's hair, and she was wearing what seemed like the exact same dress that she must have modeled for the artwork. Laura, on the other hand, knew instantly that Christean could not see, but was more interested in the tingle she felt when Christean's hand had touched her shoulder.

"I'm Laura and this is my friend, Mr. B. You and

your statue are very beautiful Christean."

"When I touch the statue's face, I can sketch it out in my mind. I can "see" other people that way too, if they let me touch their facial features. I heard you say that her eyes could see into your soul, and I was thinking how ironic that was," she said still smiling.

Laura said, "You said I could touch the eyes of the real thing. May I?"

Barto jerked his head and looked at Laura, who returned his glance with a smile and then looked back at Solomon Jarrett's daughter.

Christean chuckled and said, "I thought I was just being clever when I said that, but I don't see why not, if I can touch your face too."

Barto watched intently as both the autistic girl and the blind girl reached up and gently explored each other's face. Laura closed her eyes and sighed as her fingertips gently touched Christean's cheeks and then lightly stroked her closed eyelids.

Christean held Laura's head in her hands and painted a mental sketch of her new friend. "You are very beautiful too Laura," and then she fell suddenly silent with her eyes closed. She slowly dropped her hands to her sides. Several moments later, Laura also dropped her hands, and then took a small step backwards into Barto's waiting arms.

Susannah and Jarrett strolled up chattering lightly and obviously enjoying their mutual conversation. "I see you've met my daughter Mr. Barto. Susannah, this is my daughter, Christean, and as I was telling you, the model for my sculpture."

Christean's eyes blinked open and she was staring at the sculpture positioned directly in front of her. She quickly crossed the barrier, scooted past her father, and reached out and touched the sculpture at its eyes.

"I can see her Father!! I can see everything!! She IS so very beautiful, everything is so very beautiful!"

Jarrett stood in frozen amazement for several moments and then took his daughter's face into his hands. "You can see? But how? This is amazing! This is wonderful!"

Barto quickly recovered from his shock, took Laura's hand, and started walking to the exit nearest the parking lot. He called softly back to Mrs. Waltman, "I'll meet you at the van ma'am."

Christean said to her father, "Laura and I were talking, and then I sketched her face with my hands, and she said she wanted to touch my eyes."

Jarrett looked up at the departing Barto and Laura just as she bumped into a chair that was directly in her path. Barto grasped Laura's hand more firmly and guided her around the people and the obstacles of the museum.

"Father, I can see your face too. I want you to show me everything!"

As Susannah started her walk following Barto and her granddaughter, she could hear a chorus from Jarrett saying, "You can see!!! You can really see!"

This was followed by Christean shouting, "Everything is so beautiful!!"

Susannah Waltman smiled the entire way back home. "That was incredible Mr. Barto, I feel blessed that I was present for that miracle." She did comment on Laura's blindness and said, "She'll be okay won't she Samuel?"

"I think so ma'am, she's always recovered before."

Laura sat quietly in the back seat, staring out the

window as if she could see everything as it flew by."

After a few contemplative moments, Barto asked, "Ma'am, I read Mr. Jarrett is an Atheist, is that right?"

"Yes he is Mr. Barto, why do you ask?"

"I guess I don't understand why God would perform a miracle for someone who doesn't even believe He exists."

"Well Samuel, for me that's an easy answer. I once heard you say that your son probably doesn't want anything to do with you, but you love him anyway, unconditionally. I believe that God created everything and everyone, and it just makes sense that He loves everyone that He created, whether they believe He exists or not. And it seems to me that all of His children would get His love and His nudges, equally and unconditionally."

When they arrived home, Mr. B took Laura into the workshop to talk to her about Christean. Her vision was now fully recovered, and she was extremely excited at what had taken place.

When they both entered the house, Mrs. Waltman was completing her "Miracle Story" to her excited daughters, and Sarah looked at Barto for a comforting sign.

Barto reassured her, "Laura is fine ma'am, she can see fine again, and she is very excited about what happened today."

Sarah was relieved and took Laura up to her room and prepared her for bedtime. She returned downstairs to animated conversations about miracles and spiritual philosophies. For her part, Sarah remained mostly quiet as she worried about what could happen to her daughter.

For Barto, there were mixed emotions about every one of Laura's miracles, and how he felt privileged to be present for every one. But he was worried for Laura too. Where were these new experiences leading and what, if anything would happen next?

Chapter 21

THE PERFECT DAY

After winter and the threat of frost had passed, Barto decided to spend some time sprucing up his Old Stone Church grounds. He had noticed that while the prisoners took good care of the mowing and trimming, they did very little to enhance the old flower beds and planters that surrounded the church and its adjacent cemetery.

For a while now, he had intended to place a few windchimes around the building, and he now expanded his plans to include some flowers and plants and also some cleanup work around the entranceway and the cemetery. He was a little embarrassed when he told the Waltmans his intentions.

"I know it sounds kind of silly to go to all that trouble for a congregation of one, huh? I just want to see what it might have looked like a hundred years ago. Surely, they planted flowers and pulled some weeds and made it nice for everyone to see and enjoy. The church has always been locked when I'm there, and I've never been inside, but I often sit in my truck or on the steps and wonder what it must have been like back then."

"That's not silly Mr. Barto," said Susannah. "When people plant flowers and make their homes look nice, they appreciate compliments from their neighbors or passers-by, but mostly they plant them for their own enjoyment. If sprucing up your church makes you happy, then that is all that really matters."

Barto appreciated Mrs. Waltman's understanding words and smiled in agreement. He let them know that he would be away most of Saturday while he tended to his church.

Sarah, spoke up and said, "I hear the weather is supposed to be nice Mr. B, perhaps you would like a little company with you. I'm sure Laura would love to see your church in the daylight, and from what you tell us about her actions in the workshop, I'll bet she could be a good helper too. And if you're interested, we could pack up a picnic so that you could enjoy a break from your project."

"That sounds great Miss Sarah. I'll ask Laura if she wants to go along, and I'll warn her that I'll put her to work," he said with a smile. "To be honest though, she has never turned down an opportunity to wake up from her dream world… and who can blame her?"

Just as everyone had suspected, Laura was excited when Barto asked her if she wanted to be his helper and companion when he visited his church. On the days leading up to the weekend, they talked and they planned their project together. Friday night in the workshop, they finished the windchimes that would be placed at the church site. Laura had seen Barto's church briefly when she and her family had visited him at Thanksgiving, but this was an opportunity to see everything in daylight.

"Thank you for inviting me to your church Mr. B. I've wanted to visit it again very much, especially in the daytime, but I didn't want to ruin your privacy at your special place."

Barto smiled inwardly at Laura's words. The Stone Church was indeed his special place, and there were certainly times when he visited and used its aura to help him through some especially tough times. Fortunately however, he made most of his visits just to enjoy the peace and calm and ambience of the surroundings.

Barto bowed slightly and talked in a more formal sounding tone. "Miss Laura, it will be my honor to have you as a guest at my church. I admit that I am very protective of it, and I keep an eye out for anyone who might do it harm, but a church should be shared. I wish more people could visit and experience the same peace and calm that I feel there. I'm especially pleased that I will get to share it with my best friend."

Laura smiled and returned the bow. "Thank you kind sir, and I'll do my best to be a big help too."

When Saturday morning finally came, Barto was up at dawn as usual and felt more excited about his day than he had in a very long time. When he came upstairs to the Waltman kitchen, coffee was made and all the Waltman women, including Laura, were already there.

Everyone seemed in a very upbeat mood as they scurried about getting things ready for the afternoon meal at the church. Susannah said excitedly, "We've packed some sandwiches, and Margaret made some excellent fruit salad. Elizabeth made some of her famous potato salad too, so you will have to be careful and not get too full, or you won't get anything done today. I made some lemonade, and we have a big container of iced water so that you can take some breaks from your project."

Sarah said a bit more seriously, "Mr. B, I really can't thank you enough for what you mean to us, but especially to Laura. I could tell she was more excited too, because she was awake before I was this morning. Maybe someday we'll all have a chance to have a picnic together, but for now, I'm very excited for Laura to get the chance to be with you at your church."

Barto put his hands on Sarah's shoulders and made sure that he made direct eye contact. "Miss Sarah, I've said this before, but I need you to know for sure. Being able to do this with Laura and having the Waltmans as my friends and my family is more than I could have ever asked for." He grabbed a bag and helped gather up the supplies. "Sometimes I think that my time with Laura is a lot like it would have been with my son."

After loading his truck, Barto and Laura drove to the hardware store and picked up a few flowering plants and potting soil for their project. Even though much of the work would involve cleaning up, planting new growth was also part of their strategy.

When they arrived at the Old Stone Church, the sun was bright, the sky was clear, and the day was perfect.

"I'm not sure it could get any better than this Little One."

"You're right about that Mr. B," Laura replied as she looked around and seemed to absorb the feel of her surroundings. Barto had referred to the perfection of the weather, but when he looked at her, he saw her close her eyes, and with her arms straight out to her sides, she started a slow twirl as she captured the moment. He knew she was appreciating the warmth from the sun, but mainly she was embracing the freedom from her dream world.

In the daylight, the church looked totally different to Laura. Of course, her only other reference was during the darkness of night. As Mr. B guided her around the flowerbeds near the front entrances, he reviewed their landscaping refurbishment plan. Laura listened as she walked, but her attention was on the glowing building itself.

In mid-sentence, Barto glanced down and saw Laura's eyes opened wide in amazement at the church. He realized how easy it was to take the subdued beauty of the building for granted, and he smiled at her wonder. When they had finished the tour around the building, Barto pointed out the church's cornerstone and proudly recited the history of the congregation.

"The original building was across the street," he said as he pointed toward the far corner of the cemetery. "It was a converted house that was made of logs. They finally built a real stone church in this spot around 1850. When they had grown so large that they needed a bigger place to worship, they hired someone to grind up the stone and make them into the church that you see here now."

Laura stared at the bright walls as the intense sunlight reflected off the recycled stone. She pointed down at the cornerstone and said, "This building was built in 1900? Your church is amazing Mr. B."

"Yes it is Little One. Now let's see if we can't spruce it up a little."

They spent the rest of the morning pulling out the weeds and cleaning out the dead leaves and broken twigs left over from winter. Barto marveled at the helpful little girl's efforts, and they both appreciated how much better the church looked without the overgrowth.

Barto suggested, "How about we have some lunch before we set up the wind chimes and plant the flowers? We should be finished in no time, especially with such a good helper by my side."

Laura blushed slightly and replied, "This is so much fun Mr. B. I'm so glad you let me come along."

Barto decided to have their lunch out front in the large grassy area between the church and the road next to the cemetery. He laid the picnic blanket next to a large bell that was located all the way out near the road.

As he and Laura were settling down with their basket and supplies, he explained, "This is the original church bell. It hung up in the tower." He pointed toward the front corner of the church. "When the prisoners did some work on the building a while back, they took it down for safety reasons, and they put it out here on display."

The bell was mounted on two brick pillars that matched the fence and gate pillars of the cemetery. The bell was etched with the name of the preacher who was assigned to the church when it was built, along with the date of the church's construction. Under the bell and surrounding the pillars was a small flowerbed with hints of life already coming up through the soil.

"There are gladiolas and some other flower bulbs planted there. We shouldn't have to do anything here except scrape away the debris. The flowers are quite spectacular."

Laura admired the flower bed, and her eyes grew especially wide when she looked up at the huge bell. "What do you think it sounded like back then Mr. B?"

Barto smiled and said, "To tell you the truth, I know what it sounded like Little One. During one of my first visits, I pulled the rope, and the bell still worked just fine. In fact, why don't you give it a try now?"

Even as she rose to her feet in the direction of the bell, Laura said excitedly, "Are you sure Mr. B, I don't want to break it." She took a tentative glance at Barto and then slowly started to reach her hand toward the large rope attached to the clapper.

"It will be fine. Besides, there's no one around except us and maybe some deer and rabbits, and I don't think they will mind."

Laura grabbed hold of the rope and pulled it firmly. The bell tone was loud and deep and seemed to echo throughout the valley. She smiled deeply as she sat back down on the blanket next to her friend. "It sounds wonderful Mr. B, almost like one big windchime." Barto smiled and nodded in agreement.

The egg salad sandwiches and all the trimmings were exceptional, and Laura and Barto had worked up quite an appetite. Barto enjoyed watching Laura as she ate while she soaked in everything around her. When she looked at the bell once more, it again reminded her of the sounds of a windchime.

"How did you get started making windchimes Mr. B?"

The question caught Barto by surprise. He smiled slightly as he looked at Laura and then gazed up into the sky.

"I once saw a picture of an old man holding up his granddaughter so she could touch a windchime's sail to make it ring. The smile on her face was as big as the smile I've seen on your face. I did some research and learned how to make them. I was hoping that one day I could share them with someone special too." He looked at Laura and said, "I guess that wish has now come true."

After gathering up the picnic remnants, Barto and Laura planted their flowers in the cement block pots lining the sidewalks and steps of the church. They also filled the pots on top of the entrance gate to the cemetery and still had enough left over to plant one in an old memorial pot next to the Barto headstones. They positioned one windchime stake next to that pot, and several more in the flowerbeds next to the church. When Laura hung the chimes, the slight breeze encouraged the chimes in their delicate song.

It was mid-afternoon when their project was complete. After filling the truck with their tools, they took the time to sit on the church steps and admire their handiwork. "I think we did good Mr. B. It looks to me like the church members could come here just like they did one hundred years ago."

"I agree Little One. I've never been inside, but from the outside, you would think that there was still an active congregation that called this their home. And maybe once in awhile, they would have a picnic too, while their children played, and the adults sat around and fixed the food and enjoyed the beautiful day."

Laura excitedly joined Barto's vision and jumped up from the steps towards the front door. He smiled as Laura spoke in a voice that mimicked her idea of a church lady one hundred years ago. "My goodness those flowers are lovely sir. They bring out the best in our church. Now I think I'll go inside and see the preacher." She pretended that she was using a cane as she walked up the steps and reached for the doorknob playfully.

When her hand touched the brass handle, she assumed that the locked door would end her show, but when she twisted the knob, it turned, and when she instinctively leaned into the door, it opened several inches until she froze in shock. "It's open Mr. B," she said in a loud whisper as she pulled back her hand like she had just been burned.

Chapter 22

A CONGREGATION OF TWO

The first time he had ever visited the Old Stone Church, Barto had marveled at the beauty and the preserved state of the old, abandoned house of worship. From the outside, he could see that each window still had their original stained glass design intact, and even though they were now covered on the outside with clear acrylic protection, he could tell they were meticulously rendered. The roof peaked high, and he assumed that the ceilings must be tall and majestic.

He had tried the front doorknob on every visit he had ever made with the hope that he could see the inside in its full glory. Every effort over the years confirmed that all the doors were locked and there was no way for him to get inside.

When Laura pushed the door open, she was afraid she had done something wrong. She looked back at Mr. B as she said, "It's open Mr. B," in a guarded voice intended not to alarm any authority that may be nearby.

Barto's first reaction was shock as he sat frozen while he tried to understand what had just happened. He recovered slightly and looked up at Laura's guilty face and smiled nervously, "It's okay Little One. The workers probably left it unlocked when they were checking out something inside."

After several moments of mutual silence, and in her same quiet voice, Laura asked the question which was on Barto's mind as well, "Do you think it would be okay if we went in Mr. B? Do you think we might get in trouble if we took a peek?"

Barto slowly stood up and stared at the open door. He had dreamed of this opportunity for many years, and now he wondered if they should indeed go inside. If they went inside, would a constable of some sort come by and yell at them to get off this private property and never come back, or what if the insides were all destroyed and decayed? After all, no one had used it for a very long time.

Calm thoughts finally came back to Barto, and he reasoned that, not only was it unlikely that anyone else would come by this holy place, the worst thing that could possibly happen would be that they would be asked to leave.

Without answering Laura directly, Barto stepped in front of the little girl and tentatively pushed the door fully open. When he saw nothing fall in from the ceiling, he was convinced that it was safe enough to take at least a few steps inside. He looked down at Laura and silently held out his hand.

They walked inside, hand in hand, and entered a small alcove with two closed swinging doors, one straight ahead and one to the left that, if Barto remembered from the outside view, would lead to the tall ceiling above what was probably the main room of worship. The alcove also had a tall ceiling with a trap door which Barto deduced was the entrance to the bell tower.

When he pushed open the door to the left, Barto did not expect the brightness that shined into the large, open room. The stained glass windows seemed to magnify the intense sunlight, and the room glowed brilliantly. He and Laura took several steps into the huge room until they stopped at the back of the dozens of rows of wooden pews that were divided down the middle with a carpeted walking aisle.

They both stood with their mouths open in awe. From their vantage point, they looked down over the seating onto the stage with the preacher's pulpit in the middle, and the piano and chorus seating to the right. There was room for well over one hundred worshipers, thought Barto, especially with the benches along the side walls. Like a little boy, he stared in awe at the seemingly thousand foot ceiling. The room was magnificent and beyond even Barto's expectations. The window paintings were glorious and clear as the day they were created.

"May I get a closer look at the windows Mr. B?" Without speaking or averting his glance from the room, Barto slowly nodded his head and began a slow walk down the middle aisle as Laura wandered closer to the side walls with the windows.

Samuel Barto could not ever remember going to church as a child, or as an adult for that matter. His parents would give every indication that they were Christians, but he didn't remember them ever going to worship on Sunday. While in the Army, he had received some pressure to go to the chapel, but he politely declined. He remembers one friend saying playfully, "I suppose if you did go to church, either it would burn down or YOU would burst into flames."

When he reached the bottom of the aisle, he noticed no fire on him and none in the church, so he took a seat on the front pew directly in front of where the preacher would normally stand. He looked over at the stained glass and nearly had to shield his eyes from the bright light. But instead, he closed his eyes and let the warm sun flow over his face. When Laura had finished her examination, she came over and sat next to him on the wooden seats.

"They're beautiful Mr. B. The whole church is so beautiful."

Barto nodded his head in agreement, but still didn't say a word. He sat and absorbed the church's radiance as he relished the special power this place had always held over him. He knew that he was home here.

After several silent moments of mutual meditation, Laura asked Barto, "Did you ever go to church Mr. B, when you were younger?"

Barto shuffled on the slick wooden seat and put his arm on the headrest behind his little friend. "I've never been a church-goer," he said. "But I'm not an atheist either," he added quickly so she didn't misunderstand. "I'm just not as sure about things as most people that come to church, but I do believe that there is Someone out there who created us and looks after us." He looked over at Laura and added, "I guess it would be hard not to believe that, now that I've met you."

Until the daylight was starting to fade, Barto and Laura sat on the pew, talking a little, but mostly, they just sat and enjoyed the special atmosphere of the old abandoned church.

Finally, Barto said, "Well Little One, I guess it's time for us to leave now before we can't see our way out.

And we wouldn't want your mother to start worrying either."

"Thank you again for bringing me along Mr. B. This has been my most wonderful day ever. Your church is a very special place."

Barto took Laura's hand, and they walked up the center aisle towards the exit.

"OUR church Laura," he said. "From now on, let's call this OUR church. I believe it now has a congregation of two."

The brightness of Laura's smile seemed to lead their way out of the darkening room.

Chapter 23

THE HORSE SHOW

Near the end of summer and before the beginning of the new school year, Rasheem saw a poster for a horse show and exhibition hosted by a Kuwaiti dignitary. He asked Elizabeth if they could go. Lately, he had shown significantly more interest in his mother's Muslim beliefs and culture. The visit by the "Angel Charles Barto" had fueled his search for more information. Elizabeth wasn't completely comfortable driving the several hours to the fairgrounds where the show was being held. She asked Barto if he and Laura would like to come along, and he could be their driver. Barto was always looking for opportunities to take Laura out into the world and experience her new awakening. Sarah was a bit tentative and naturally worried about her daughter's well-being, but she knew that Barto was a capable guardian, and she wanted Laura to experience life as much as was reasonably possible.

During the two hour drive to the horse show, an

excited Rasheem asked Barto about his experiences in the Gulf War. From Elizabeth, he already knew why there was a war, and he knew that the United States and many other countries had joined forces to remove the invaders of Kuwait and give the country back to its citizens.

"I remember being very busy when we got there, and we waited and hoped that we didn't have to fight. Just like everyone else, we watched the news and hoped the talks would result in an answer without going to war." Barto drove quietly for a bit as the war's memories hit him in the face. "In the beginning, we were rushing to get over there and getting set up for the possibility of a fight. Then we waited and grew bored during the months of ongoing negotiations." He remembered the daily rumors that always raised their hopes and then the disappointment when they turned out to be false.

"There were times during the wait that we got a chance to go downtown and shop and eat a restaurant meal. I used to watch the families walking hand in hand in the malls. That's what made me miss home the most."

Rasheem said, "The kids at school say that girls are treated badly by Muslims because boys are superior in their culture."

"I had heard a little about that too, before I went there, but when I saw them, I knew that the parents loved their children very much, both boys and girls. I made friends with a guard in the Saudi Army, and he had two daughters. He congratulated me for having a son, but when he talked about his daughters, his eyes lit up, and he always smiled when he spoke about them. He explained to me that the reason that women are covered and protected is because Muslims hold their women in such high esteem."

When they arrived at the Capitol fairgrounds, the

show was just beginning, and Prince Ahmad Al-Aziz and his assistants were putting on quite an impressive display. Their horses were huge and decorated in silks and coins. The Prince was obviously a professional and a very good statesman for his native country. After their part of the show was complete, other horses and riders from the United States and many other countries took their turns. The Prince remained with his horses in the stable area and proudly answered any questions that visitors might have had.

Rasheem asked, "Can we go down and see the horses up close Elizabeth?"

"I don't see why not," she answered, and they all made their way down to the stables.

When they got close to the Prince, Elizabeth introduced Sergeant Barto as a veteran of the Persian Gulf War. The Prince seemed very grateful as he vigorously shook Barto's hand. "My father served in the war of our country's liberation when I was just a young boy. I am very honored to meet you Sergeant Barto. I am honored to have received my college education here in the United States, and I feel fortunate that my daughter has lived most of her life here with me." Barto later learned that the Prince had married an American woman he had met while going to school.

Elizabeth next introduced the Prince to Rasheem while telling him about Rasheem's background. "His mother was Muslim, and he is interested in learning more about the Muslim faith and culture."

A very gracious Prince Al-Aziz shook Rasheem's hand intently and with a broad smile said, "Allah willing, you will learn all about his love and greatness. Come, let me introduce you to my daughter. She is your age and she might be able to answer some questions peer to peer."

They walked several stalls over to where several handlers and a beautiful smiling girl about Rasheem's age were talking to and brushing a magnificent show horse.

"Jessica, I'd like you to meet my new friends. This is Sergeant Barto, Miss Elizabeth, Rasheem, and Miss Laura. Rasheem may have some questions later about our celebration as Muslims." Rasheem took a small step forward and bowed as he shook her hand. He barely noticed that she was sitting in a wheelchair.

"I am very pleased to meet you all. Rasheem, please ask me anything, and I'll be happy to share my love for Allah."

The Prince said, "Miss Elizabeth, with your blessing, I have a gift I would like to give Rasheem. I would like to give him a token of his visit today that will also help him explore his interest in learning more about our culture." When Elizabeth agreed, the Prince invited them to his trailer and suggested that Barto could stay with Jessica and the horses. Barto agreed as he wanted to stay with the horses and look for an opportunity for Laura to experience some of the show.

Soon after Elizabeth, the Prince, and Rasheem had departed, Barto tentatively stroked the nose of the beautiful horse.

"Would you like to groom him Laura?" Jessica asked as she held out her brush to Laura.

Before Barto could explain to Jessica that Laura could not answer, Laura spoke up and said, "Thank you Jessica. That would be wonderful. He is very beautiful."

Barto quietly stared with great interest as Jessica transferred the brush to Laura's hand, and their fingers touched.

It was Laura who yelped and dropped the brush. "Oooh, I'm so clumsy," she said as she reached down and picked up the brush. The tingle when they touched had startled her, and when she stood back upright, she looked up at Barto with a smile before turning her full attention back to Jessica.

"Did you have an accident while you were riding a horse Jessica?" Laura asked.

"Not at all Laura, I've never been able to walk or ride a horse, but I hope to one day, Allah willing."

Laura slowly sank to her knees in front of the wheelchair and asked, "May I touch your legs Jessica?"

With a smile down to the kneeling Laura, Jessica answered, "Of course you can, but they are quite a bit skinnier than most girls our age."

Laura lifted Jessica's long skirt slightly and gently grabbed her ankles in each hand. Barto watched intently as Laura closed her eyes and slumped slightly. Jessica inhaled a deep breath and barely whispered, "Oh my," as she too closed her eyes. After several moments, Laura dropped her hands to her sides, but remained kneeling in front of Jessica.

"Look what I have Mr. Barto!" said an excited Rasheem as he led Elizabeth and Prince Al-Aziz back to the stables. "The Prince gave me a prayer rug and a Quran."

Barto gave Rasheem a quick glance and with a polite smile, said "Nice!"

Elizabeth added, "The Prince is very generous…" and she stopped as she noticed Laura on her knees next to Jessica in her wheelchair.

The Prince noticed the pause and looked over at his daughter just as she was opening her eyes. "Is everything okay Jessica?"

"My legs feel funny Father," she answered slowly. "They FEEL funny Father!" she said excitedly. "I feel my legs! Father, I feel my legs!" Jessica scrunched forward and firmly grasped the arms of her chair.

"Now be careful, don't..." the Prince stopped in mid-sentence as he reached for her.

She stood upright with no more assistance than her hand on her father's arm for balance. Without a word, she took a tentative step forward, and with her father hovering over her, she took another step, and then another. "I'm walking Father!!" she exclaimed as she turned back around. "I'm walking Father! I can walk!" She took several slow steps back and shoved the chair back and out of her way.

When she turned back around, her father was on his knees with his arms outstretched like a parent coaxing his infant for her first steps. Jessica took several slow but confident steps until she and her father met with a hug.

"Praise Allah!" the Prince kept repeating as he held her tight and tears of joy formed in his eyes. "Praise Allah! Praise Allah!"

Laura had remained silent in her kneeling position, staring blankly with her ever present smile still on her face. Barto recovered from the shock of Jessica's walk and bent down and picked Laura up in his arms and cradled her like a newborn baby. "Miss Elizabeth, we'll meet you in the van." With Laura still cradled in his arms, Barto started walking towards the fairgrounds' exit and the parking lot. Elizabeth was still in shock from the recent events and grabbed Rasheem's hand as she nodded after Barto.

"We were talking and Laura asked if she could touch my legs," Jessica said to her father. "And then you came back, and I could feel my legs... and now I can walk!"

Prince Al-Aziz was still crouched and hugging his

daughter when he looked up at Elizabeth with a huge smile and said, "Praise Allah," once again.

Elizabeth was still watching Barto and Laura walking away. The Prince followed her gaze and saw Barto walking away and through the crowds with Laura cradled in his arms.

"Can I ride with you Father, please?" asked Jessica. "It is Allah's will that I can walk; surely it is His will that I ride."

The Prince turned back to his daughter, and with a loud joyous voice shouted, "Praise to Allah, my daughter can walk, and now she will ride!" The Prince's horse was already saddled, and he mounted him smoothly. With the help of his assistants, Jessica grabbed his outstretched hand and was pulled into the saddle in front of her father. They rode and rode until the horse finally needed rest.

As Rasheem and Elizabeth walked hand in hand back to the van, Rasheem could barely contain himself. "That was amazing Elizabeth," said an excited Rasheem. "Allah did this, didn't He? I saw it with my own eyes! Allah must be powerful and loving to have done a miracle like this, don't you think?"

"Most definitely Rasheem," replied a smiling Elizabeth. "Most definitely indeed."

Chapter 24

DEAR DIARY

Every chance they had, Barto and Laura would sit in the workshop at the long table and read the stories that Sarah had enjoyed as a young girl. Laura remained enthusiastic, and Barto was inspired by her excitement and sense of accomplishment. Every day they read, he would report back to the Waltmans with assurance that she was learning very quickly.

They progressed through the initial large stack of books, and soon she was going through more from the house's library that were bigger and more advanced. By winter, she was mostly reading to Barto on her own, with only the occasional stutter when she came across a word or phrase that she needed his help with.

Barto would stand at his workbench for hours and enjoy Laura's voice as she became more and more confident as a storyteller. When she had read through all the appropriate aged books at the Waltman house, Barto asked Sarah if he and Laura could start going to the county library and let her pick out some additional reading.

"Certainly Mr. B," she replied with a smile. "But at this rate, she'll be reading better than me in no time."

"I think she's already reading better than me," replied Barto as he returned her smile.

Barto tried to time his visits to the library so that there were less people looking through the shelves. He wasn't sure exactly how her dream world worked, but he knew for sure that she would be awake if it were just Laura and he alone at a location.

Laura loved the library and practically ran through the aisles with amazement at the endless number of stories that were available to her. There were so many books to choose from. She had trouble picking out the five that the library had limited them to check out at one time.

Barto explained, "As soon as we finish these first five, we'll bring them back and get five more. And we can keep doing that until you've read them all."

"There's so many to choose from Mr. B, it's hard for me to decide."

Barto and Laura became regular visitors to the library as she progressed quickly through each visit's selections. On one such visit, Barto noticed Laura frequently glancing across the room to an older lady who was writing notes down in a wire bound notebook.

After Barto explained to her that the lady was probably reading some information from the stories and then writing down reminder notes, Laura nodded her head in understanding. "Maybe one day I will learn to write well, and I can write notes and maybe even write my own stories."

On her next visit to Poppy's workshop, Laura

found an assortment of pencils and several writing tablets on the reading table. Barto explained to her that she was now reading so well, it was time she learned how to write well too. "Besides," he said, "I can't wait to read one of YOUR stories."

Laura learned to write even faster than she had learned to read. Barto started out by having her copy words from her books into her notebook. Eventually, he had her start writing down some of her own thoughts and assigned her the task of creating and writing down some simple stories of her own.

Very quickly, she had progressed to the point that she was now able to put together a few random thoughts of her own and write them in her notebook. He could see that she was getting more and more confident every day. Although she was nervous about the concept, Barto was hoping that her writing skills would soon be good enough so that she could communicate with her mother and her family.

When Barto handed her a wrapped present in the shape of a book, Laura was excited and wondered out loud, "A new book, thank you Mr. B, I wonder what it could be?"

Barto watched her as she opened the gift and frowned slightly as she scanned the pages of blank paper. "It's a diary Little One. Every day you can write down your thoughts of what happened that day, or what you wish would happen, or anything that comes to your mind. Your diary can become your own private place where you can write down anything you want, and no one else needs to know."

"But I can't write that well yet Mr. B. I'm afraid I won't do very well."

"You can start out slow with just a few words if

you like. No one else will see, not even me. Then you can practice more and more until you get very good. Before too long, you'll be writing out your whole day." Barto demonstrated how she might like to start her pages every day and how she might like to end them. He explained that she could do them any way she wanted, but reminded her that the middle part with her thoughts was the most important.

Laura understood. When she knew it was getting close to the time she would go back into the house, she quickly pulled out her diary to make her first entry. Barto didn't seem to notice as he was occupied with one of his tools on the far side of the shop.

Dear Diary,

Today was a very good day.

-----Laura

Chapter 25

A REASON TO LIVE,
A REASON TO DIE

Samuel Barto was hoping that today's visit to the VA hospital would be his last scheduled visit that had resulted from his self-inflicted wound. He hoped there would be no more pills and no more therapy. His leg was healed, and his mind was somewhat stable.

Susannah, Sarah, and Laura were coming along to visit with the hospital's Assistant Administrator, Doctor Daniel Keefer. He was in the Army the same time as Susannah's husband, and was the physician who had worked with Laura when she was first diagnosed with autism. He was obviously quite fond of Laura as they had connected, even if she couldn't talk. They were hoping he could see a change in Laura and maybe help her to get to the next level of consciousness.

When they arrived at the hospital, Barto's appointment went quickly, and he indeed was given a clean bill of health. They all walked together and arrived at Dr. Keefer's office five minutes before their scheduled appointment.

"We're here to see Dr. Keefer. We have an appointment," said Susannah. The receptionist looked frazzled, but politely asked them to have a seat while she called the doctor. A few minutes later, a doctor came in through the hallway entrance, but it was not Dr. Keefer.

"I'm Dr. Arbuckle, and I'll be seeing Dr. Keefer's scheduled patients today."

Susannah spoke up pleasantly, "We're old friends of Dr. Keefer, I hope he's feeling well."

"Come with me please," he answered as he led them to a quiet cove down the hallway. "I'm sorry Mrs. Waltman, Dr. Keefer passed away earlier today. He had a heart attack last night and never recovered."

Susannah and Sarah covered their mouths in shock and anguish while Dr. Arbuckle helped them sit in a couple of nearby chairs. Barto reached out for Laura's hand, but she was not at his side or anywhere in sight. He realized that in the shock of the moment, she must have been left behind. Without alarming the already upset Waltmans, he checked the office they had been in and then started walking down the hallway looking for her.

"Mommy!" Barto heard Laura scream.

He quickly found the room from which the scream had originated, and he found Laura inside. Dr. Daniel Keefer was still lying in the hospital bed he had been in since he had been admitted as a patient last night. He was no longer hooked up to the monitoring equipment, and there were neither IVs nor oxygen tubes running from his body. He looked like a man who was lying on his back, taking a nap. Barto noticed his shirt was open, and his chest was bare. He even imagined he could sense a slight rise of his chest from the intake of a breath, but knew that was impossible.

Laura was lying in a heap at the side of Dr. Keefer's bed and was not moving. Barto leaned over her and could see that she was unconscious and was not breathing. Her hands were stiff and spread, indicating to Barto that she must have visited Dr. Keefer and put her hands on his chest. He distinctly heard Keefer take a breath and glanced up to see him open his eyes and stare at the ceiling.

"Oh Little One," he cried as he looked back at the crumpled and still figure of the young girl. As tears started to form in his eyes, he slowly reached down to cup her cheek. When he touched her face, he felt a sharp tingle and recoiled in shock and surprise.

Down the hallway, Sarah had heard Laura's scream, and even though she had never heard Laura speak, she instinctively knew it was the voice of her daughter. Her head jerked immediately towards the sound, and she quickly got up and ran towards the voice. She didn't have the benefit of being near the sound of Laura's scream like Barto, so it took a few door openings and subsequent apologies before she entered Dr. Keefer's room. Keefer was still lying in his bed, but his eyes were open, and they seemed to indicate that he was coming out of a daze. Barto was on his knees next to the bed and was staring at both of his hands as he held them, palms up and straight out. He looked over at Sarah as she entered, and she saw the tears and shock in his eyes and confusion on his face. Laura was lying next to Barto in a lifeless pile at the side of the bed. Sarah also saw that she was not breathing.

As she slowly glided to Laura's side, Sarah said, "Oh Laura," and collapsed to her knees in a slow and agonizing motion. Tears quickly formed in her eyes as she looked up and saw Dr. Keefer taking in breath and realized that Laura must have touched him back to life. It seems that it had cost her, her own life.

As she slowly reached down to stroke her daughter's face, Barto quickly but gently grabbed Sarah's hand before it could touch Laura's skin. Sarah stopped and looked into Barto's eyes and thought it odd how he was looking back, now with a slight smile on his face.

Without a word, he took her still outstretched wrist into both of his hands, and after turning it over, he maintained eye contact while he kissed the back of her hand. When he released her wrist, she slowly retracted her hand but never stopped looking into his eyes.

Barto continued smiling as he looked back down at his best friend. He remembered his most recent conversation with his father when he said, "It can be a fine line between a reason to live and a reason to die." He also remembered the conversation with Sarah outside his bedroom door. "Take care of our little girl Mr. B," she had said, and he had promised her that he would.

Susannah Waltman had finally located her daughter. When she entered the room, she was overcome with the sight of Dr. Keefer slowly reviving and of Laura in an unmoving heap on the floor. She could say nothing as she simply stared and held her hands up to her face in shock.

Barto slowly reached down to Laura and embraced her face with both of his hands. The tingle was back, and even though he could feel it course through his fingers and up his arms, he wasn't surprised this time. He felt a warmth race down his arms and through his body, and he closed his eyes to accept it in. Then there was darkness and sleep as he slowly slumped against the bed rails and onto the floor.

For several moments, Sarah and Susannah both stayed perfectly still in stunned silence, anticipating and hoping for some sort of sign from Laura and Barto.

Finally, Laura's eyes fluttered, and she sucked in a deep breath of air. Sarah reached for her daughter and held her head up with one hand while stroking her cheek with the other. Laura's eyelids opened fully, and she looked directly into her mother's eyes.

Dr. Keefer remembered the pain and the pressure and the nurses and doctors scurrying around him, and that's when he had fallen into darkness. A short time ago, he had awoken from the deepest sleep he could ever remember. It was so deep a sleep that it had taken him a while to regain his senses and any movement at all, once he was awake. At first, he could hear a bit of activity around him, but could not turn his head towards the noise until his friend, Susannah Waltman, walked into the room with a shocked look on her face. When he was able, he turned and looked at the side of the bed where he saw Susannah's daughter Sarah, kneeling next to her unmoving autistic daughter Laura. An unknown man was reaching down towards Laura and took her face in his hands. Soon thereafter, Dr. Keefer heard Laura speak for the first time.

"Mommy," she said clearly to her mother, and she smiled up into her eyes. Sarah started to cry even more as she looked down into her daughter's eyes; eyes that were clear and full of recognition.

"Laura," she answered back as she hugged her daughter close to her and they shared a deep embrace.

Laura returned her mother's hug with a huge smile. Her head was comfortably positioned on her mother's shoulder as she looked up at her grandmother, who was also crying tears of joy.

"Hello Grandmother."

Susannah quickly cleared her throat and wiped a few tears from her eyes. "Hello Granddaughter," she replied with an attempt of composure that failed when she started to laugh lightly and cry some more.

Laura looked over and saw Mr. B lying slumped on the floor against the bed. He actually seemed comfortable, and it even seemed like he was smiling slightly, but Laura and everyone else in the room saw that he wasn't breathing. She abruptly released her mother and shuffled over to Barto. "Mr. B, please Mr. B!" she cried out. She looked down at her hands and then reached down to hold his face. She felt no tingle and no life at all. "Please Mr. B," she repeated and then looked up at her mother, and then to her grandmother, and then to Dr. Keefer with pleading eyes. "Please!" she said to the room as she looked back down at Barto with her tear-filled eyes.

A group of nurses and doctors rushed into the room, and after hesitating with shock as they saw a revived Dr. Keefer, they stepped in to administer treatment to Barto. They immediately directed the family to a nearby waiting room and put Barto into the bed that Keefer had recently risen from.

In the waiting room, all three Waltmans went back and forth from joy and sorrow as Laura was talking and coherent, but with concern for Barto's condition.

"Mommy, Mr. B has to be okay," she said. "He has to be." She looked up at Susannah and said, "Please Grandmother, please tell me Mr. B will be okay."

"I don't know Laura," she answered as she sat down next to her newly animated granddaughter and hugged her to her chest. "But no matter what happens, it does look like he has left a little bit of himself with you."

"You can talk Laura," said Sarah. "You can hear us, and you can understand us, and you can talk to us. And you have such a lovely voice, just like Mr. B said you did."

Val and his family were notified and they rushed to the hospital, closely followed by his other two sisters and Rasheem. For the next several hours, all of the Waltmans were content to sit and stare in amazement at the newly energized Laura. She sat and talked to her mother, her grandmother, and the rest of her family as if she had been communicating with them all her life. But there still was a level of concern while they waited for word of Mr. Barto's condition.

Finally, it was Dr. Keefer that came into the waiting room, looking to talk with the Waltmans. Susannah said, "You should be resting Daniel and certainly not wandering around the hospital."

"I feel fine Susannah, I don't know how, but I do." He looked over at Sarah and Laura and continued, "I feel like I owed it to you to look after Mr. Barto."

"Is Mr. B going to be okay?" asked Laura.

"I'm sorry Laura, Mr. Barto has passed away. I don't think he suffered when he passed though, he almost seemed like he was smiling a bit, but there was nothing more we could do."

Chapter 26

THE BEGINNING

Dear Diary,

Aunt Margaret and Aunt Elizabeth are funny. They don't let anyone else call them by their nicknames except me. With stern and serious faces, they both tell me, "Laura, you can call us 'Aunt Maggie' and 'Aunt Lizzie', but no one else can." And then they break out in a big smile. I love talking to them so much. They must think I'm a chatterbox.

Uncle Valentine is simply Uncle Val. Nothing else would suit him. He helps me out with so many things, sort of like Mr. B used to do. He tells me he is trying to find a new caretaker for the "Waltman Estate", but we both know there will never be another Mr. B.

Grandmother Waltman says it doesn't matter to her what I call her, but she told me once that all her children used to call her mother "Nana" so that's what I call her now. I think that deep down, she really likes that.

She is smart and kind, and she really knows how to cook. Even now, she hugs me so hard sometimes, I can barely breathe, but I don't mind. I know that she hugs me tight because she loves me very much. I also love her very much, so I hug her back real tight too.

Some people think that if you call your mother 'Mommy', you're acting like a big baby, but that's what I called her in my mind when I couldn't speak to her, and calling her that now just feels right. Mommy told me today that Aunt Maggie would be starting my piano lessons tomorrow. She said that today, we would start celebrating the start of my new life, and music was always a big part of the past and would be a big part of our future.

It has been more than a year now since Mr. B passed away, and I woke up from my dream world. Nana often reminds me that Mr. B may be gone, but part of him is still here in me.

This morning, we went to the dedication of the new Veteran's Center, and I got the chance to be with my new friends. Mayor Ruben Houser gave a speech and introduced the new "Samuel Barto Veteran's Center". He praised all the people responsible for making it happen. Mayor Houser's brother had died in Vietnam and in his honor, his mommy cut the big ceremonial ribbon to invite people in the building for the first time. Mrs. Houser's ankle seemed much better than when Mr. B and Mommy and I saw her at the cemetery.

Inside the Center, Miss Harriet sang a song that made many people cry. Aunt Maggie assured me that they were tears of joy. She told me that Miss Harriet knew a lot of important people when she was in the Air Force, and she talked to them and got them to approve and support this new Veteran's Center. Her granddaughter

Lydia is one of my new best friends, and she starts taking piano lessons with me tomorrow. She can hear very well now, and one day, she wants to play a song while her Grandma Harriet sings.

Aunt Lizzie told me that Prince Al-Aziz heard about the need for the Center, and he donated a lot of money to help build it. His daughter told Rasheem that they had lots of money, and as a good Muslim, her father wanted to help out the veterans, like Mr. B, who helped free his country. Jessica can walk and ride really well now. She even invited me to visit her and ride some horses with her one day.

Nana showed me the statue of a military man at the front of the building and explained to me that Mr. Jarrett not only made the statue, he helped design and lay out the entire building. He wanted Nana to hang her painting of Mr. B inside, but Nana said that his portrait would be hung up at home with the rest of our family. So instead, Mr. Jarrett's daughter, Christean, painted a really big Mural for the wall of the Center. She sees really good now, and she is becoming a very good artist, just like her daddy.

The final speech of the morning was given by the new Administrator of the Veteran's Center. As soon as the Vet Center project was approved and funded, Dr. Keefer agreed to help run the entire place. He had all of the necessary experience, and he was feeling much better now since the day he got sick when we were at the hospital.

I really liked seeing the new building and my friends, but I was getting anxious to go out to Mr. B's church and see my present to him. Soon after the dedication ceremony, we drove out to the church so that we could see his new bench, and I could talk to him like I have done many times since he has been gone.

There weren't nearly as many people at the church as there were at the Veteran's Center this morning, but there were still quite a few that wanted to come by. Mommy said she recognized some of them, but we didn't know many of them. She said that they all had stopped by to pay their respects to Mr. B.

Uncle Val was already at the church when we got there. When the small crowd had gathered around him in the cemetery, he dedicated a new bench with a little plate on it that had Mr. B's engraved name and his date of birth and the date he died. Mr. B had wanted his ashes scattered in the cemetery, so my uncle took care of that before a lot of people came today. He explained to everyone how this church and cemetery now had a new caretaker for ever and ever.

Earlier, Uncle Val had hung my present to Mr. B on a tree limb hanging over Mr. B's bench. I made him a butterfly windchime that had "Mr. B" burnt on one side and "Nudged" on the other. Next to the bench, Uncle Val had planted a Persian Gulf War veteran memorial marker that held an American Flag.

Earlier in the week, I had asked Mommy if it was okay if we took Mr. B's Heart Pot to his church, and she thought that was a great idea. Uncle Val had brought it out a few days ago and had put it right next to the flag. The plant in the pot had wilted, just like the day Mommy had given it to him, but she and I promised each other that we would visit again soon with a new one.

When Uncle Val had finished talking around the bench, our group slowly made its way to the church parking lot where we all mingled and talked. Honestly, I hoped that we wouldn't be there too long, because it was getting close to dark, and I still wanted to talk to Mr. B before we went home.

Our family was the focus of the crowd, and one by one, each family and individual came over to us to shake our hands, give their regards, and sometimes share a story. Sheriff Bastian was there and he gave hugs to everyone, and an especially big one to Nana. He assured us that he would come by the church quite often to help Mr. B keep an eye on things. Benjamin Shaffer and his family were there too, and he talked about Mr. B's friendship with his daddy. We didn't know most of the rest of the visitors, and they didn't have a whole lot to say. Most of them said they had simply come by to pay their respects to Mr. B.

It was getting nearer to sunset when the last family approached our group. Mommy told me to calm down because I was getting "antsy", but I was anxious to revisit Mr. B's bench without the formality of the crowd.

The final family was a younger man, his wife, and a pretty little girl who looked about 3 years old. Nana told me that the man looked very familiar, but she could not recall from where, and she hoped she didn't embarrass herself to the man with her "Old Lady's incomplete memory."

The man stepped forward and reached out his hand to her and said, "Thank you for allowing us to be here with you today Mrs. Waltman. I heard about the Veteran's Center dedication on the news, and we overheard a few people talking about this ceremony."

Nana smiled as she took his hand and said, "Don't be silly, you are most certainly welcome here, did you know Mr. Barto?"

"No ma'am, at least not much that I can remember, but I wish I had. This is my wife Maria and my daughter Rebecca. My name is Adam Barto. I'm

Samuel Barto's son."

We all stopped talking, and Nana froze in shock, still with Adam's hand in hers. Our entire family turned their now silent faces towards the Barto family. After several silent moments, Rebecca looked up at her father and said, "Is there something wrong Daddy?"

Before he could answer her, we all came out of our daze at the same time. Nana pulled Adam's hand and arm towards her and gave him a huge hug. "Oh, Mr. Barto!! Nothing is wrong at all. We are so glad you're here!"

Uncle Val took his turn shaking Adam's hand, and my aunts took turns hugging Maria and fussing over Mr. B's granddaughter. I adopted Rebecca as my new best friend right then and there.

Nana said, "Your father was a very special man Mr. Barto, I hope you'll let us tell you all about him."

"I'd like that very much ma'am."

I was excited too, and I said to Mommy, "Can we show Rebecca Mr. B's windchime?" We all felt very comfortable as our two families were holding hands and chatting as we slowly walked over to Mr. B's bench and gazed up at the windchime. There was no breeze blowing to give the chime its sound, so I stood up on the bench and pushed the butterfly so that the chime sounded. Rebecca's face lit up, and Adam picked her up so that she could also push the butterfly and make the chime sing.

As the remaining light started to fade, we all agreed to go back to the "Waltman Estate" and talk about so many things. As we started towards the parking lot, I asked Mommy if I could stay behind at the bench for just a few more minutes to say goodbye to Mr. B.

"You're son is here Mr. B, and he is such a nice man! And your granddaughter is here too, she is very pretty. I'm going to tell her everything about you and how you were my Nudge. I hope you like the windchime I made for you. Uncle Val helped me burn in the words on the sail. I asked Mommy if it was okay if we brought your Heart Pot out here to keep you company. The plant isn't so good, but we'll bring you a new one when we visit you again soon. I promise to come back often, and I'll keep it well."

I reached down and adjusted the pot on its pedestal and stroked the poor wilted plant like I remembered doing in the workshop on the first day I became awake when I was alone with Mr. B. I turned around to go back to my family, but after a few small footsteps, I slowly turned and looked at the bench. "I can never thank you enough Mr. B; thank you for being my Nudge." A sudden light wind picked up, and the butterfly windchime sang deep and bright.

The air always seems cleaner here. I close my eyes and lean back my head, breathing in the cool breeze as it caresses my face. The chimes sing loudly as they sway in the wind. I feel awake and alive, and I embrace the joy of my whole new world. This is my beginning.

When I open up my eyes, I glance down at the Heart Pot and notice its plant is now completely healthy with a big yellow flower in full bloom. A beautiful Monarch butterfly is flapping its wings as it sits on the flower, drinking in its nectar. I smile big and let out a quiet, but knowing chuckle.

Satisfied, I turn and find myself skipping my way back to my family and my new found friends. Maybe Mr. B's granddaughter would like to learn how to make her own butterfly windchime.

-----Laura

ACKNOWLEDGMENT

Special thanks to Sonnette Harris, Debbi Niklaus Sebring, Dwight Harris, Terri Niklaus Driscoll, and Kevin Harris who provided immeasurable encouragement and support through all of the seemingly impossible times.
...and without whom, I would no longer exist.